HORRiD HENRY'S
Dreadful
Deeds

Francesca Simon

HORRiD HENRY'S Dreadful Deeds

Illustrated by Tony Ross

Orion
Children's Books

**For the lovely original cast of Horrid Henry Live and Horrid!
(and all our good times…)**

Steven Butler	*Horrid Henry*
Stephen McGill	*Horrid Henry Too*
Rachael Swift	*Moody Margaret*
Alex Tregear	*Perfect Peter*
Philip Bosworth	*Dad*
Ruth Calkin	*Rabid Rebecca*
Clark Devlin	*Weepy William*
Howie McCullough	*Aerobic Al*
Katy Porrett	*Sour Susan*

This collection first published in Great Britain in 2009
by Orion Children's Books
a division of the Orion Publishing Group Ltd
Orion House
5 Upper Saint Martin's Lane
London WC2H 9EA
An Hachette UK Company

1 3 5 7 9 10 8 6 4 2

ISBN 978 1 84255 721 1

Printed in Italy by Printer Trento

www.horridhenry.co.uk
www.orionbooks.co.uk

Contents

Horrid Henry's Grisly Gallery

Blood Boil Bob

Lisping Lily

Santa

Mrs Mossy

Mr Mossy

Maggie

HORRID HENRY'S
Sleepover

Horrid Henry loved sleepovers. Midnight feasts! Pillow fights! Screaming and shouting! Rampaging till dawn!

The time he ate all the ice cream at Greedy Graham's and left the freezer door open! The time he jumped on all the beds at Dizzy Dave's and broke them all. And that time at Rude Ralph's when he – well, hmmn, perhaps better not mention that.

There was just one problem. No one would ever have Horrid Henry at their house for a sleepover more than once. Whenever Henry went to sleep at a friend's house, Mum and Dad were sure to get a call at three a.m. from a demented parent screaming at them to pick up Henry immediately.

Horrid Henry couldn't understand it. Parents were so fussy. Even the parents of great kids like Rude Ralph and Greedy Graham. Who cares about a little noise? Or a broken bed? Big deal, thought Horrid Henry.

It was no fun having friends sleep over at his house. There was no rampaging and feasting at Henry's. It was lights out as usual at nine o'clock, no talking, no feasting, no fun.

So when New Nick, who had just joined Henry's class, invited Henry to stay the night, Horrid Henry couldn't believe his luck. New beds to bounce on. New biscuit tins to raid. New places to rampage. Bliss!

Henry packed his sleepover bag as fast as he could. Mum came in. She looked grumpy.

'Got your pyjamas?' she asked.

Henry never needed pyjamas at sleepovers because he never went to bed.

'Got them,' said Henry. Just not with him, he thought.

'Don't forget your toothbrush,' said Mum.

'I won't,' said Horrid Henry. He never forgot his toothbrush – he just chose not to bring it.

Dad came in. He looked even grumpier.

'Don't forget your comb,' said Dad.

Horrid Henry looked at his bulging backpack stuffed with toys and comics. Sadly, there was no room for a comb.

'I won't,' lied Henry.

'I'm warning you, Henry,' said Mum. 'I want you to be on best behaviour tonight.'

'Of course,' said Horrid Henry.

'I don't want any phone calls at three a.m. from Nick's parents,' said Dad. 'If I do, this will be your last sleepover ever. I mean it.'

NAG NAG NAG.

'All right,' said Horrid Henry.

Ding dong.

A woman opened the door. She was wearing a Viking helmet on her head and long flowing robes. Behind her stood a man in a velvet cloak holding back five enormous, snarling black dogs.

wOOF wOOF wOOF wOOF wOOF

'TRA LA LA BOOM-DY AY,' boomed a dreadful, earsplitting voice.

'Bravo, bravo!' shouted a chorus from the sitting room.

GRRRRRRR! growled the dogs.

Horrid Henry hesitated. Did he have the right house? Was New Nick an alien?

'Oh don't mind us, dear, it's our opera club's karaoke night,' trilled the Viking helmet.

'Nick!' bellowed the Cloak. 'Your friend is here.'

Nick appeared. Henry was glad to see he was not wearing a Viking helmet or a velvet cloak.

'Hi Henry,' said New Nick.

'Hi Nick,' said Horrid Henry.

A little girl toddled over, sucking her thumb.

'Henry, this is my sister, Lily,' said Nick.

Lily gazed at Horrid Henry.

'I love you, Henwy,' said Lisping Lily. 'Will you marry with me?'

'NO!' said Horrid Henry. Uggh. What a revolting thought.

'Go away, Lily,' said Nick.

Lily did not move.

'Come on, Nick, let's get out of here,' said Henry. No toddler was going to spoil his fun. Now, what would he do first, raid the kitchen, or bounce on the beds?

'Let's raid the kitchen,' said Henry.

'Great,' said Nick.

'Got any good sweets?' asked Henry.

'Loads!' said New Nick.

Yeah! thought Horrid Henry. His sleepover fun was beginning!

They sneaked into the kitchen. The floor was covered with dog blankets, overturned food bowls, clumps of dog hair, and gnawed dog bones. There were a few suspicious looking puddles. Henry hoped they were water.

'Here are the biscuits,' said Nick.

Henry looked. Were those dog hairs all over the jar?

'Uh, no thanks,' said Henry. 'How about some sweets?'

'Sure,' said Nick. 'Help yourself.'

He handed Henry a bar of chocolate. Yummy! Henry was about to take a big bite when he stopped. Were those – teeth marks in the corner?

'**Raaa!**' A big black shape jumped on Henry, knocked him down, and snatched the chocolate.

Nick's dad burst in.

16

'Rigoletto! Give that back!' said Nick's dad, yanking the chocolate out of the dog's mouth.

'Sorry about that, Henry,' he said, offering it back to Henry.

'Uhh, maybe later,' said Henry.

'Okay,' said Nick's dad, putting the slobbery chocolate back in the cupboard.

Eeew, gross, thought Horrid Henry.

'I love you, Henwy,' came a lisping voice behind
him. 'AH HA HA HA HA HA HA HA!'
warbled a high, piercing voice from the sitting room.
Henry held his ears. Would the windows shatter?
'Encore!' shrieked the opera karaoke club.
'Will you marry with me?' asked Lisping Lily.
'Let's get out of here,' said Horrid Henry.

Horrid Henry leapt on Nick's bed.
Yippee, thought Horrid Henry. Time to get
bouncing.

Bounce — CRASH!

The bed collapsed in a heap.
'What happened?' said Henry. 'I hardly did
anything.'
'Oh, I broke the bed ages ago,' said Nick. 'Dad said
he was tired of fixing it.'

Rats, thought Henry. What a lazy dad.

'How about a pillow fight?' said Henry.

'No pillows,' said Nick. 'The dogs chewed them.'

Hmmn.

They could sneak down and raid the freezer, but for some reason Henry didn't really want to go back into that kitchen.

'I know!' said Henry. 'Let's watch TV.'

'Sure,' said New Nick.

'Where is the TV?' said Henry.

'In the sitting room,' said Nick.

'But – the karaoke,' said Henry.

'Oh, they won't mind,' said Nick. 'They're used to noise in this house.'

'DUM DUM DE DUM DUMM DUM DE DUM DUMM DUM –'

Horrid Henry sat with his face pressed to the TV. He couldn't hear a word Mutant Max was shrieking with all that racket in the background.

'Maybe we should go to bed,' said Horrid Henry, sighing. Anything to get away from the noise.

'Okay,' said New Nick.

Phew, thought Horrid Henry. Peace at last.

SNORE! SNORE!

Horrid Henry turned over in his
sleeping bag and tried to get comfortable. He hated
sleeping on the floor. He hated sleeping with the
window open.

He hated sleeping with the radio on. And he hated
sleeping in the same room with someone who snored.

Awhooooooo! howled the winter wind through
the open window.

SNORE!
SNORE!

'I'm just a lonesome cowboy, lookin' for a
lonesome cowgirl,' blared the radio.

WOOF WOOF WOOF barked the dogs.

'Yeowwwwww!' squealed Henry, as five wet, smelly dogs pounced on him.

'Awhoooo!' howled the wind.

SNORE!

SNORE!

'TOREADOR – on guard!' boomed the opera karaoke downstairs.

Horrid Henry loved noise. But this was – too much.

He'd have to find somewhere else to sleep.

Horrid Henry flung open the bedroom door.

'I love you, Henwy,' said Lisping Lily.

Slam! Horrid Henry shut the bedroom door.

Horrid Henry did not move.

Horrid Henry did not breathe.

Then he opened the door a fraction.

'Will you marry with me, Henwy?'

Aaarrrgh!!!

Horrid Henry ran from the bedroom and barricaded himself in the linen cupboard. He settled down on a pile of towels.

Phew. Safe at last.

'I want to give you a big kiss, Henwy,' came a little voice beside him.

NOOOOOOOO!

It was three a.m.

'TRA LA LA
BOOM-DY AY!'

'— LONESOME COWBOY!'

SNORE!
SNORE!

AWHOOOOOOOOOOOOOO!

WOOF! WOOF! WOOF!

Horrid Henry crept to the hall phone and dialled his number.

Dad answered.

'I'm so sorry about Henry, do you want us to come and get him?' Dad mumbled.

'Yes,' wailed Horrid Henry. 'I need my rest!'

HORRiD HENRY
and the Dinner Guests

FIZZ! POP! GURGLE! BANG!

Horrid Henry sat on the kitchen floor watching his new Dungeon Drink kit brew a bubbly purple potion.

BELCH! CRUNCH! OOZE! SPLAT!

Beside it, a Grisly Ghoul Grub box heaved and spewed some Rotten Crispies.

Dad dashed into the kitchen.

'Want a crisp?' said Henry, smirking.

'No!' said Dad, putting on his apron. 'And I've told you before to play with those disgusting kits in your bedroom.'

Why Henry's grandmother had bought him those terrible toys for Christmas he would never know.

'Henry, I want
you to listen carefully,' said
Dad, feverishly rolling out pastry.
'Mum's new boss and her husband are coming to
dinner in an hour. I want total cooperation and perfect
behaviour.'

'Yeah, yeah,' said Henry, his eyes glued to the
frothing machine.

Horrid Henry's parents didn't have guests for
dinner very often. The last
time they did Henry had
sneaked downstairs, eaten
the entire chocolate cake
Dad had baked for dessert
and then been sick all
over the sofa. The time
before that he'd put
whoopee cushions on
all the guests' seats,

PRRRRRP

bitten Peter, and broken the banister by sliding down it.

Dad started getting pots and pans down.

'What are you cooking?' said Perfect Peter, tidying up his stamps.

'Salmon wrapped in pastry with lime and ginger,' said Dad, staring at his list.

'Yummy!' said Perfect Peter. 'My favourite!'

'Yuck!' said Horrid Henry. 'I want pizza. What's for pudding?'

'Chocolate mousse,' said Dad.

'Can I help?' said Peter.

'Of course,' said Mum, smiling. 'You can pass round the nuts and crisps when Mr and Mrs Mossy arrive.'

Nuts? Crisps? Henry's ears perked up.

'I'll help too,' said Henry.

Mum looked at him. 'We'll see,' she said.

'I don't think Henry should pass round the nuts,' said Peter. 'He'll only eat them himself.'

'Shut up, Peter,' snarled Henry.

'Mum! Henry told me to shut up!' wailed Peter.

'Henry! Stop being horrid,' muttered Dad, grating ginger and squeezing limes.

While Dad rolled up salmon in pastry, Mum dashed about setting the table with the best china.

'Hey! You haven't set enough places,' said Henry. 'You've only set the table for four.'

'That's right,' said Mum. 'Mrs Mossy, Mr Mossy, Dad and me.'

'What about me?' said Henry.

'And me?' said Peter.

'This is a grown-ups' party,' said Mum.

'You want me . . . to go . . . to bed?' Henry stuttered. 'I'm not . . . eating with you?'

'No,' said Dad.

'It's not fair!' shrieked Henry. 'What am I having for supper then?'

'A cheese sandwich,' said Dad. 'We've got to get ready for the guests. I'm already two minutes behind my schedule.'

'I'm not eating this swill!' shrieked Henry, shoving the sandwich off his plate. 'I want pizza!'

'That's all right, Dad,' said Peter, tucking into his sandwich. 'I understand that grown-ups need to be by themselves sometimes.'

Henry lunged at Peter. He was a cannibal trussing his victim for the pot.

'AAARGHH!' shrieked Peter.

'That's it, Henry, go to bed!' shouted Mum.

'I won't!' screamed Henry. 'I want chocolate mousse!'

'Go upstairs and stay upstairs!' shouted Mum.

Ding dong!

'Aaagh!' squealed Dad. 'They're early! I haven't finished the mousse yet.'

Horrid Henry stomped upstairs to his bedroom and slammed the door.

He was so angry he could hardly speak. The injustice of it all. Why should he go to bed while Mum and Dad were downstairs having fun and eating

chocolate mousse? The delicious smell of melting
chocolate wafted into his nostrils. Henry's tummy
rumbled. If Mum and Dad thought he'd stay in bed

while they all had fun downstairs they had rocks for brains.

SCREEEECH! SCREEEECH!

Perfect Peter must be playing his cello for Mum and Dad and the guests. Which meant . . . Horrid Henry smiled. The coast was clear. Hello, nuts, here I come, thought Henry.

Henry tiptoed downstairs. The screechy-scratchy sounds continued from the sitting room.

Horrid Henry sneaked into the empty kitchen. There were the bowls of nuts and crisps and the drinks all ready to serve.

Cashews, my favourite. I'll just have a few, he thought.

Chomp. Chomp. Chomp.

Hmmn, boy, those nuts were good. Irresistible, really, thought Henry. A few more would go down a treat. And, if he poured the remaining nuts into a smaller bowl, no one would notice how many he'd eaten.

CHOMP! CHOMP! CHOMP!

Just one more, thought Henry, and that's it.

Horrid Henry swizzled his fingers round the nut bowl.

Uh-oh. There were only three nuts left.

Yikes, thought Henry. Now I'm in trouble.

FIZZ! POP! GURGLE! BANG! BELCH! CRUNCH! OOZE! SPLAT!

Horrid Henry looked at his Grisly Grub box and Dungeon Drink kit and bopped himself on the head. What an idiot he was. What better time to try out his grisly grub than . . . now?

Henry examined the Rotten Crispies he'd made earlier. They looked like crisps, but certainly didn't taste like them. The only problem was, what to do with the good crisps?

Yum yum! thought Henry, crunching crisps as fast as he could. Then he refilled the bowl with Rotten Crispies.

Next, Henry poured two frothing dungeon drinks into glasses, and put them on the tray.

Perfect, thought Henry. Now to make some Nasty Nuts to replace all those cashews.

The kitchen door opened. Dad came in.

'What are you doing, Henry? I told you to go to bed.'

'Mum said I could serve the nuts,' said Henry, lying shamelessly. Then he grabbed the two bowls and escaped.

The sound of applause came from the sitting room. Perfect Peter bowed modestly.

'Isn't he adorable?' said Mrs Mossy.

'And so talented,' said Mr Mossy.

'Hello, Mr and Mrs Bossy,' said Henry.

Mum looked horrified.

'Mossy, not Bossy, dear,' said Mum.

'But that's what you call them, Mum,' said Henry, smiling sweetly.

'Henry is just going to bed,' said Mum, blushing.

'No I wasn't,' said Henry. 'I was going to serve the nuts and crisps. Don't you remember?'

'Oooh, I love nuts,' said Mrs Mossy.

'I told you to stay upstairs,' hissed Mum.

'Muuuum,' wailed Peter. 'You said I could serve the guests.'

'You can serve the crisps, Peter,' said Henry graciously, handing him the bowl of Rotten Crispies. 'Would you like a cashew, Mrs Bossy?'

'Mossy!' hissed Mum.

'Ooh, cashews, my favourite,' said Mrs Mossy. She plunged her fingers into the mostly empty nut bowl, and finally scooped up the remaining three.

Henry snatched two back.

'You're only supposed to have one nut at a time,' he said. 'Don't be greedy.'

'Henry!' said Mum. 'Don't be rude.'

'Want a nut?' said Henry, waving the bowl in front of Mr Mossy.

'Why, yes, I . . .' said Mr Mossy. But he was too late. Henry had already moved away to serve Mum.

'Want a nut?' he asked.

Mum's hand reached out to take one, but Henry quickly whisked the bowl away.

'Henry!' said Mum.

'Do have some crisps, Mrs Mossy,' said Perfect Peter. Mrs Mossy scooped up a large handful of

Rotten Crispies and then stuffed them in her mouth.

Her face went purple, then pink, then green.

'BLECCCCCH!' she spluttered, spitting them out all over Mr Mossy.

'Peter, run and get Mrs Mossy something to drink!' shouted Mum.

Peter dashed to the kitchen and brought back a frothing drink.

'Thank you,' gasped Mrs Mossy, taking the glass and gulping it down.

'YUCK!' she spluttered, spitting it out. 'Are you trying to poison me, you horrible child?' she choked, flailing her arms and crashing into Dad, who had just walked in carrying the drinks tray.

CRASH! SPLASH!

Mum, Dad, Peter, and Mr and Mrs Mossy were soaked.

'Peter, what have you done?' shouted Mum.

Perfect Peter burst into tears and ran out of the room.

'Oh dear, I'm so sorry,' said Mum.

'Never mind,' said Mrs Mossy, through gritted teeth.

'Sit down, everyone,' said Henry. 'I'm going to do a show now.'

'No,' said Mum.

'No,' said Dad.

'But Peter did one,' howled Henry. 'I WANT TO DO A SHOW!'

'All right,' said Mum. 'But just a quick one.'

Henry sang. The guests held their ears.

'Not so loud, Henry,' said Mum.

Henry pirouetted, trampling on the guests.

'Ooof,' said Mr Mossy, clutching his toe.

'Aren't you finished, Henry?' said Dad.

Henry juggled, dropping both balls on Mrs Mossy's head.

'Ow,' said Mrs Mossy.

'Now I'll show you my new karate moves,' said Henry.

'NO!' shouted Mum and Dad.

But before anyone could stop him Henry's arms and legs flew out in a mad karate dance.

'HI-YA!' shrieked Henry, knocking into Mr Mossy.

Mr Mossy went flying across the room.

Whoosh! Off flew his toupee.

Click-clack! Out bounced his false teeth.

'Reginald!' gasped Mrs Mossy. 'Are you all right? Speak to me!'

'Uggghhh,' groaned Mr Mossy.

'Isn't that great?' said Henry. 'Who wants to go next?'

'What's that terrible smell?' choked Mrs Mossy.

'Oh no!' screamed Dad. 'The salmon is burning!'

Mum and Dad ran into the kitchen, followed by Mr and Mrs Mossy.

Smoke poured from the oven. Mum grabbed a tea towel and started whacking the burning salmon.

WHACK! THWACK!

'Watch out!' screamed Dad.

The towel thwacked the bowl of chocolate mousse and sent it crashing to the ground.

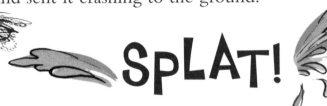

SPLAT!

There was chocolate mousse on the floor. There was chocolate mousse on the ceiling. And there was chocolate mousse all over Mr and Mrs Mossy, Mum, Dad and Henry.

'Oh no,' said Mum, holding her head in her hands. Then she burst into tears. 'What are we going to do?'

'Leave it to me, Mum,' said Horrid Henry. He marched to the phone.

'Pizza Delight?' he said. 'I'd like to order a mega-whopper, please.'

Poor Mr Mossy has lost his toupee. What style should he wear next?

POP! GURGLE! FIZZ!

BANG! OOZE! BELCH!

CRUNCH! SPLAT!

Dungeon Drink Recipe
Beetroot juice
Mushroom Soup
Cola
Bits of liquorice
Lots of Tabasco Sauce
Chilli powder

The
GOO-SHOOTER
CHAMPION!

The BEST!

UNBEATABLE!

A STAR!

FABULOUS!

The
ICE-CREAM
EATING KING!

HENRY
A STAR IS BORN

HORRID HENRY
Minds his Manners

'Henry and Peter! You've got mail!' said Mum.

Henry and Peter thundered down the stairs.
Horrid Henry snatched his letter and tore open the
green envelope. The foul stink of mouldy socks wafted
out.

Yo Henry!
Marvin the Maniac here. You sound
just like the kind of crazy guy we
want on GROSS-OUT! Be at TV
Centre next Saturday at 9.00 a.m.
and gross us out! It's a live
broadcast, so anything can happen!
Marvin

'I've been invited to be a contestant on *Gross-Out*!' screamed Henry, dancing up and down the stairs. It was a dream come true. 'I'll be shooting it out with Tank Thomas and Tapioca Tina while eating as much ice cream as I can!'

'Absolutely not!' said Mum. 'You will not go on that disgusting show!'

'Agreed,' said Dad. 'That show is revolting.'

'It's meant to be revolting!' said Horrid Henry. 'That's the point.'

'N–O spells no,' said Mum.

'You're the meanest, most horrible parents in the whole world,' screamed Henry. 'I hate you!' He threw himself on the sofa and wailed. **'I WANT TO BE ON *GROSS-OUT*! I WANT TO BE ON *GROSS-OUT*!'**

Perfect Peter opened his letter. The sweet smell of lavender wafted out.

Dear Peter,
what a wonderful letter you wrote
on the importance of perfect manners!
As a reward I would like to invite
you to be my special guest on the live
broadcast of MANNERS WITH MAGGIE
next Saturday at TV Centre at 9:00
a.m.

You will be showing the girls and
boys at home how to fold a hankie
perfectly, how to hold a knife and fork
elegantly, and how to eat spaghetti
beautifully with a fork and spoon.

I am very much looking forward to
meeting you and to enjoying your lovely
manners in person.
Sincerely,
Maggie.

'I've been invited to appear on *Manners With Maggie!*' said Peter, beaming.

'That's wonderful, Peter!' said Mum. She hugged him.

'I'm so proud of you,' said Dad. He hugged him.

Horrid Henry stopped screaming.

'That's not fair!' said Henry. 'If Peter can be on his favourite TV show why can't I be on mine?'

Mum and Dad looked at each other.

'I suppose he does have a point,' said Dad. He sighed.

'And we don't have to tell anyone he's on,' said Mum. She sighed.

'All right, Henry. You can be a contestant.'

'YIPPEE!' squealed Henry, stomping on the sofa and doing his victory jig. 'I'm going to be a star! *Gross-Out* here I come!'

The great day arrived at last. Horrid Henry had been practising so hard with his Goo-Shooter he could hit Perfect Peter's nose at thirty paces. He'd also been practising shovelling ice cream into his mouth as fast as he could, until Mum caught him.

Perfect Peter had been practising so hard folding his hankie that he could do it with one hand. And no one could

twirl spaghetti with a spoon as beautifully or hold a
knife and fork as elegantly as Perfect Peter.

At nine a.m. sharp, Mum, Henry, and Peter walked
into TV Centre. Henry was starving. He'd skipped
breakfast, to have more room for all the ice cream
he'd be gobbling.

Horrid Henry wore old jeans and dirty trainers.
Perfect Peter wore a jacket and tie.

A woman with red hair and freckles rushed up to
them with a clipboard.

'Hi, I'm Super Sally. Welcome
to TV Centre. I'm sorry boys,
we'll have to dash, we're
running late. Come with me
to the guests' waiting room.
You're both on in five
minutes.'

'Can't I stay with
them?' said Mum.

'Parents to remain
downstairs
in the parents'
room,' said Super
Sally sternly. 'You
can watch on the
monitors there.'

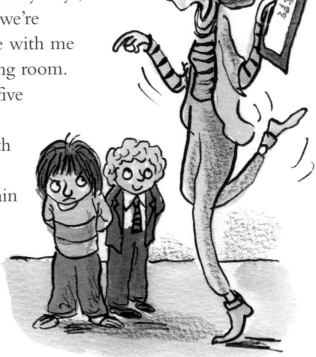

'Good luck, boys,' said Mum, waving.

Sally stared at Peter as they hurried down the hall.

'Aren't you worried about getting those smart clothes dirty?' said Sally.

Peter looked shocked.

'I never get my clothes dirty,' he said.

'There's always a first time,' chortled Sally. 'Here's the waiting room. Studios one and two where you'll be filming are through those doors at the end.'

In the room was a sofa and two tables. One, marked *Gross-Out*, was groaning with sweets, crisps and fizzy drinks.

The second, labelled *Manners with Maggie*, was laid with a crisp white cloth. A few dainty vegetables were displayed on a china plate.

Horrid Henry suddenly felt nervous. Today was his day to be a TV star! Had he practised enough? And he was so hungry! His stomach tightened.

'I need a wee,' said Horrid Henry.

'Toilets next door,' said Super Sally. 'Be quick. You're on in one minute.'

Perfect Peter didn't feel in the least nervous. Practice made perfect, and he knew he was. What disgusting food, he thought, wandering over to the *Gross-Out* table.

A man wearing combat fatigues dashed into the room.

'Ah, there you are!' he boomed. 'Come along! It's your big moment!'

'I'm ready,' said Peter, waving his handkerchief.

The man pushed him through the door marked Stage 1.

Henry returned.

A lady in high heels and a pearl necklace poked her head round the door.

'You're on, dear!' said the lady. 'Goodness, you look a little untidy. Never mind, can't be helped.' And she ushered Henry through the door marked Stage 2.

Henry found himself on a brightly lit stage. He blinked in the brilliant lights.

'Let's give a warm welcome to today's guest!' cried a voice. A *female* voice.

The studio audience exploded into applause.

Henry froze. Who was that woman?

Where was Marvin the Maniac?

Something's wrong, he thought. This was not the set of *Gross-Out*. It was a pink and yellow kitchen. Yet it looked vaguely familiar ...

Meanwhile, on Stage 1, Perfect Peter shrank back in horror as two gigantic children carrying Goo-Shooters and massive bowls of ice cream advanced towards him. A presenter, laughing like a hyena, egged them on.

'You're not Maggie!' said Peter. 'And I don't know how to use a—'

'Get him guys!' squealed Marvin the Maniac.

'HELLLLP!' shrieked Peter.

Back on Stage 2, Henry suddenly realised where he was.

'Now don't be shy, darling!' said the presenter, walking quickly to Henry and taking him firmly by the hand. 'Peter's here to show us how to fold a hankie and how to eat beautifully!' It was Maggie. From *Manners with Maggie.*

What could Henry do? He was on live TV! There were the cameras zooming in on him. If he screamed there'd been a terrible mistake that would ruin the show. And hadn't he heard that the show must go on? Even a dreadful show like *Manners with Maggie*?

Henry strolled onto centre stage, smiling and bowing.

'Now Peter will show us the perfect way to fold a hankie.'

Horrid Henry felt a sneeze coming.

'AAAACHOOO!' he sneezed. Then he wiped his nose on his sleeve.

The audience giggled. Maggie looked stunned.

'The . . . hankie,' she prompted.

'Oh yeah,' said Henry, feeling in his pockets. He removed

a few crumpled wads of ancient tissue.

'Here, use mine,' said Maggie smoothly.

Henry took the beautifully embroidered square of silky cloth and scrunched it into a ball. Then he stuffed it into his pocket.

'Nothing to it,' said Henry. 'Scrunch and stuff. But why bother with a hankie when a sleeve works so much better?'

Maggie gulped. 'Very funny, Peter dear! We know he's only joking, don't we, children! Now we'll show the girls and boys—'

But Horrid Henry had noticed the table, set with a chocolate cake and a large bowl of spaghetti. Yummy! And Henry hadn't eaten anything for ages.

'Hey, that cake looks great!' interrupted Henry. He dashed to the table, dug out a nice big hunk and shoved it in his mouth.

'Stop eating!' hissed Maggie. 'We haven't finished the hankie demonstration yet!'

But Henry didn't stop.

'Yummy,' he said, licking his fingers.

Maggie looked like she was going to faint.

'Show the girls and boys how to use a knife and fork elegantly, Peter,' she said, with gritted teeth.

'Nah, a knife and fork slows you down too much. I *always* eat with my fingers. See?'

Horrid Henry waved his chocolate-covered hands.

'I'm sure it was just the excitement of being on TV that made you forget to offer me a slice of cake,' prompted Maggie. She gazed in horror at the cake, now with a gaping hole on the side.

'But I want to eat it all myself!' said Horrid Henry. 'I'm starving! Get your own cake.'

'Now I'm going to teach you the proper way to eat spaghetti,' said Maggie stiffly, pretending she hadn't heard. 'Which we should have done first, of course, as we do not eat dessert before the main course.'

'I do!' said Henry.

'Hold your spoon in your left hand, fork in your right, pick up a teensy tiny amount of spaghetti and twirl twirl twirl. Let's see if my little helper can do it. I'm sure he's been practising at home.'

''Course,' lied Henry. How hard could it be to twirl spaghetti? Henry picked up his spoon, plunged his fork into an enormous pile of spaghetti and started to twirl. The spaghetti flew round the kitchen. A few strands landed on Maggie's head.

'Whoops,' said Henry. 'I'll try again.' Before Maggie
could stop him he'd seized another huge forkful.

'It keeps falling off,' said Henry. 'Listen, kids, use
your fingers – it's faster.' Then Henry scooped a
handful of spaghetti and crammed it into his mouth.

'It's good,' mumbled Henry, chewing loudly with
his mouth open.

'Stop! Stop!' said Maggie. Her voice rose to a
polite scream.

'What's wrong?' said Henry, trailing great strings of
spaghetti out of his mouth.

Suddenly Henry heard a high-pitched howl. Then Perfect Peter burst onto the set, covered in green goo, followed by whooping children waving Goo-Shooters.

'Maggie! Save me!' shrieked Peter, dropping his shooter and hurling himself into her arms. 'They're trying to make me eat between meals!'

'Get away from me, you horrible child!' screamed Maggie.

It was the Goo-Shooter gang at last! Better late than never, thought Henry.

'Yeee haaa!' Henry snatched Peter's Goo-Shooter, jumped onto the table and sprayed Tapioca Tina, Tank

Thomas and most of the audience. Gleefully, they returned fire. Henry took a step back, and stepped into the spaghetti.

SPLAT!

'Help!' screamed Maggie, green goo and spaghetti dripping from her face.

'Help!' screamed Peter, green goo and spaghetti dripping from his hair.

'CUT!' shouted the director.

Horrid Henry was lying on the comfy black chair flicking channels. Sadly, *Manners with Maggie* was no longer on TV since Maggie had been dragged screaming off the set. *Mischief with Mildred* would be on soon. Henry thought he'd give it a try.

Hey TV people:

Now that you've dumped Manners with Maggie, I've got a great idea: Manners with **Henry**! This would be much more fun. I would show everyone how to slurp spaghetti; how to chew with their mouth open; the fastest way to eat with your fingers; how to slouch and eat; why you should never use a fork again; 10 tips for belching; and why you should never say Please or thank you.

From
Henry

HORRID HENRY'S
Revenge

SLAP!

'Waaaaaaaaaa!'

SLAP! SLAP! PINCH!

'Muuuummmmmm!' shrieked Peter. 'Henry slapped me!'

'Did not!'

'Did too! And he pinched me!'

'Stop being horrid, Henry!' said Mum.

'But Peter started it!' shouted Henry.

'Did not!' wailed Peter. 'Henry did!'

Horrid Henry glared at Perfect Peter.

Perfect Peter glared at Horrid Henry.

Mum went back to writing her letter. Horrid Henry lashed out and pulled Peter's hair. He was a coiling cobra unleashing his venom.

'**E**owwwwww!' shrieked Peter.

'Go to your room, Henry!' screamed Dad. 'I've had just about enough of you today!'

'Fine!' shouted Henry. 'I hate you, Peter!' he shrieked, stomping up to his bedroom and slamming the door as loud as he could.

It was so unfair! Peter was never sent to his room. Horrid Henry was sent to his so often he might as well live there full-time. Henry couldn't burp without Peter trying to get him into trouble.

'Mum! Henry's dropping peas on the floor!'

'Dad! Henry's sneaking sweets!'

'Mum! Henry's eating on the new sofa!'

'Dad! Henry's playing on the phone!'

Horrid Henry had had enough. He was sick and tired of that goody-goody ugly toad tattle-tale brat.

But what could he do about Peter? He'd tried selling him as a slave to Moody Margaret, but Henry didn't think she'd buy him again. If only he knew how to cast spells, he could turn Peter into a toad or a beetle or a worm. Yes! Wouldn't that be great! He'd charge everyone 10p to look at his brother, the worm. And if Peter-worm ever wriggled out of line he'd be fish bait. Horrid Henry smiled.

Then he sighed. The truth was, he was stuck with Peter. But if he couldn't sell Peter, and he couldn't turn Peter into a worm, he could get Peter into trouble.

Unfortunately, getting Perfect Peter into trouble was easier said than done. Peter never did anything wrong. Also, for some reason he didn't always trust Henry. The only way to get Peter into trouble was to trick him. And if it took all year, Horrid Henry vowed he would come up with a perfect plan. A plan to get Peter into trouble. Big, big, BIG trouble. That would be almost as good as turning him into a worm.

'I'll pay you back, Peter,' growled Henry, thumping his teddy, Mr Kill, against the bedpost. 'I will be revenged on you!'

'What are you doing, Henry?' asked Peter.

'Nothing,' said Horrid Henry. Quickly he stopped poking around the old apple tree at the end of the garden and stood up.

'You're doing something, I know you are,' said Peter.

'Whatever I'm doing is none of your business, telltale,' said Henry.

'Have you found something?' said Peter. He looked at the base of the tree. 'I don't see anything.'

'Maybe,' said Henry. 'But I'm not telling you. You can't keep a secret.'

'Yes I can,' said Peter.

'And you're too young,' said Henry.

'No I'm not,' said Peter. 'I'm a big boy. Mum said so.'

'Well, too bad,' said Horrid Henry. 'Now go away and leave me alone. I'm doing something important.'

Perfect Peter slunk off about ten paces, then turned and stood still, watching Henry.

Horrid Henry continued to prowl around the tree, staring intently at the grass. Then he whistled and dropped to his knees.

'What have you found?' said Perfect Peter eagerly. 'Treasure?'

'Much better than treasure,' said Horrid Henry. He picked something up and hid it in his hand.

'Oh show me,' said Peter. 'Please. Oh please!'

Horrid Henry considered.

'If – and I mean if – I tell you something, do you swear by the sacred oath of the Purple Hand to say nothing about this to anyone?'

'I swear,' said Peter.

'Even if you're being tortured by aliens?'

'I WON'T TELL!' shrieked Peter.

Horrid Henry put his finger to his lips, then tiptoed away from the tree to his fort. Peter followed.

'I don't want them to know I'm telling you,' he whispered, when they were hidden behind the branches. 'Otherwise they'll disappear.'

'Who?' whispered Peter.

'The fairies,' said Henry.

'Fairies,' squeaked Perfect Peter. 'You mean you've seen—'

'Shh!' hissed Horrid Henry. 'They'll run away if you tell anyone.'

'I won't,' said Perfect Peter. 'Promise. Oh wow, fairies! In our garden! Oh, Henry! Fairies! Just wait till I tell my teacher.'

'NO!' screamed Horrid Henry. 'Tell no one. Especially grown-ups. Fairies hate grown-ups. Grown-ups stink to fairies.'

Perfect Peter clasped his hand over his mouth.

'Sorry, Henry,' he said.

Horrid Henry opened his hand. It was sprinkled with gold glitter.

'Fairy dust,' said Horrid Henry.

'It looks just like glitter,' said Perfect Peter.

'Of course it looks like glitter,' said Horrid Henry. 'Where do you think glitter comes from?'

'Wow,' said Peter. 'I never knew glitter came from fairies.'

'Well now you know,' said Henry.

'Can I see them, Henry?' asked Peter. 'Please let me see them!'

'They only come out to dance at dead of night,' said Horrid Henry.

'Past my bedtime?' said Perfect Peter.

'Course,' said Horrid Henry. 'Midnight is the fairy hour.'

'Oh,' said Peter. His face fell.

'Told you you were too young,' said Henry.

'Wait,' said Perfect Peter. 'If they only come out at midnight, how come you've seen them?'

'Because I've sneaked out and hidden up the apple tree,' said Horrid Henry. 'It's the only way.'

'Ah,' said Perfect Peter. 'Umm,' said Perfect Peter. 'Ooh,' said Perfect Peter.

'I'm going to see them tonight,' said Henry casually.

'Do you think you could ask them to come before seven-thirty?' said Peter.

'Oh yeah, right,' said Henry. ' "Hiya, fairies! My brother wants you to dance for him at seven o'clock." "Sure thing, Henry," ' said Henry in a high squeaky fairy voice. 'You don't speak to fairies. You have to hide up the tree. If they knew I'd seen them they'd run away and never come back.'

Perfect Peter was in torment. He wanted to see the fairies more than anything in the world. But getting

out of bed after lights out! And sneaking outside! And
climbing the tree! And on a school night! It was too
much.

'I can't do it,' whispered Perfect Peter.

Henry shrugged. 'Fine, baby. You need your rest.'

Peter hated being called baby. Next to 'smelly
nappy', it was the worst name Henry could call him.

'I am not a baby.'

'Yes you are,' said Henry. 'Now go away, baby. Just
don't blame me when you spend the rest of your life
moaning that you missed seeing real live fairies.'

Horrid Henry started to leave the fort.

Perfect Peter sat very still. Fairies! But was he brave
enough, and bad enough, to sneak out of the house –
at night?

'Don't do it,' whispered his angel.

'Do it,' squeaked his devil, a very small, sad, puny creature who spent his life inside Peter's head squashed flat by the angel.

'I'll come,' said Perfect Peter.
YES! thought Horrid Henry.
'Okay,' said Henry.

Tiptoe. Tiptoe.
 Tiptoe. Tiptoe.
  Tiptoe. Tiptoe.

Horrid Henry sneaked down the stairs. Perfect Peter followed him. Softly, Henry opened the back door, and slipped outside. He held a small torch.

'It's so dark!' said Perfect Peter, staring into the shadows at the bottom of the garden.

'Quiet,' whispered Horrid Henry. 'Follow me.'

They crept across the lawn down to the apple tree. Perfect Peter looked up into the ghostly branches.

'It's too high for me to climb,' he protested.

'No it isn't, I'll give you a leg up,' said Horrid Henry. He grabbed Peter and shoved him up. Peter caught the lowest branch and started to climb.

'Higher,' said Henry. 'Go as high as you can.'

Peter climbed. And climbed. And climbed.

'This is high enough,' squeaked Perfect Peter. He settled himself on a branch, then cautiously looked down. 'I don't see anything,' he whispered.

There was no reply.

'Henry?' said Peter.

'Henry!' said Peter, a little louder.

Still there was no reply. Perfect Peter peered into the darkness. Where could he be? Could Henry have been kidnapped by fairies? Oh no!

Then Perfect Peter saw a dreadful sight.

There was his brother, darting back into the house!

Perfect Peter did not understand. Why wasn't Henry waiting to see the fairies? Why had he left Peter?

And then suddenly Peter realised the terrible truth. His treacherous brother had tricked him.

'I'll get you – you're gonna be in big trouble – I'll – I'll— ' squeaked Peter. Then he stopped. His legs were too short to reach the lower branch.

Perfect Peter couldn't climb down. He was stuck up a tree, all alone, at night. He had three choices. He could wait and hope that Henry would come back and help him. Fat chance. Or he could sleep all night in the damp, cold, scary, spooky tree. Or he could—

'MUUUUUUUM!' screamed Peter. 'DAAAADD!'

Mum and Dad stumbled out into the darkness. They were furious.

'What are you doing out here, Peter!' screamed Mum.

'You horrible boy!' screamed Dad.

'It was Henry's fault!' shrieked Peter, as Dad helped him down. 'He brought me here! He made me climb up.'

'Henry is sound asleep in bed,' said Mum. 'We checked on the way out.'

'I am so disappointed in you, Peter,' said Dad. 'No stamp collecting for a month.'

'WAAAAAAAH!' wailed Peter.

'Shuddup!' screamed the neighbours. 'We're trying to sleep.'

Meanwhile, back in bed, Horrid Henry stretched and smiled. No one could pretend to be asleep better than Horrid Henry.

What a perfect revenge, he thought. Peter in trouble. Henry in the clear. He was so excited he never noticed his torn, dirty, leafy clothes.

Unfortunately, the next morning, Mum did.

Perfect Peter's Top Secret Fairy Notes

What to do when you meet a fairy

1. Fairies are shy, so always whisper
2. Walk on tiptoe
3. Dress up as one yourself
4. Cover yourself in glitter
5. Choose a fairy name for yourself like Blossom

Remember, Fairy Liquid is not for fairies!

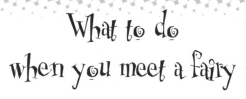

HORRID HENRY'S
Wedding

'm not wearing these horrible clothes and that's that!'

Horrid Henry glared at the mirror. A stranger smothered in a lilac ruffled shirt, green satin knickerbockers, tights, pink cummerbund tied in a floppy bow and pointy white satin shoes with gold buckles glared back at him.

Henry had never seen anyone looking so silly in his life.

'Aha ha ha ha ha!' shrieked Horrid Henry, pointing at the mirror.

Then Henry peered more closely. The ridiculous-looking boy was him.

Perfect Peter stood next to Horrid Henry. He too was smothered in a lilac ruffled shirt, green satin knickerbockers, tights, pink cummerbund and pointy white shoes with gold buckles. But unlike Henry, Peter was smiling.

'Aren't they adorable?' squealed Prissy Polly. 'That's how my children are always going to dress.'

Prissy Polly was Horrid Henry's horrible older cousin. Prissy Polly was always squeaking and squealing:

'Eeek, it's a speck of dust.'

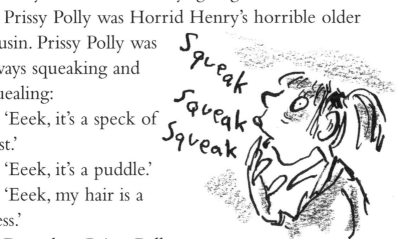

'Eeek, it's a puddle.'

'Eeek, my hair is a mess.'

But when Prissy Polly announced she was getting married to Pimply Paul and wanted Henry and Peter to be pageboys, Mum said yes before Henry could stop her.

'What's a pageboy?' asked Henry suspiciously.

'A pageboy carries the wedding rings down the aisle on a satin cushion,' said Mum.

'And throws confetti afterwards,' said Dad.

Henry liked the idea of throwing confetti. But carrying rings on a cushion? No thanks.

'I don't want to be a pageboy,' said Henry.

'I do, I do,' said Peter.

'You're going to be a pageboy, and that's that,' said Mum.

'And you'll behave yourself,' said Dad. 'It's very kind of cousin Polly to ask you.'

Henry scowled.

'Who'd want to be married to *her*?' said Henry. 'I wouldn't if you paid me a million pounds.'

But for some reason the bridegroom, Pimply Paul, did want to marry Prissy Polly. And as far as Henry knew, he had not been paid one million pounds.

Pimply Paul was also trying on his wedding clothes. He looked ridiculous in a black top hat, lilac shirt, and a black jacket covered in gold swirls.

'I won't wear these silly clothes,' said Henry.

'Oh be quiet, you little brat,' snapped Pimply Paul.

Horrid Henry glared at him.

'I won't,' said Henry. 'And that's final.'

'Henry, stop being horrid,' said Mum. She looked

extremely silly in a big
floppy hat dripping
with flowers.

Suddenly
Henry grabbed at
the lace ruffles round
his throat.

'I'm choking,' he
gasped. 'I can't breathe.'

Then Henry fell to the
floor and rolled around.

'Uggggghhhhhhh,' moaned
Henry. 'I'm dying.'

'Get up this minute, Henry!' said Dad.

'Eeek, there's dirt on the floor!' shrieked Polly.

'Can't you control that child?' hissed Pimply Paul.

'I DON'T WANT TO BE A PAGEBOY!' howled Horrid Henry.

'Thank you so much for asking me to be a pageboy, Polly,' shouted Perfect Peter, trying to be heard over Henry's screams.

'You're welcome,' shouted Polly.

'Stop that, Henry!' ordered Mum. 'I've never been so ashamed in my life.'

'I hate children,' muttered Pimply Paul under his breath.

Horrid Henry stopped. Unfortunately, his pageboy clothes looked as fresh and crisp as ever.

All right, thought Horrid Henry. You want me at the wedding? You've got me.

Prissy Polly's wedding day arrived. Henry was delighted to see rain pouring down. How cross Polly would be.

Perfect Peter was already dressed.

'Isn't this going to be fun, Henry?' said Peter.

'No!' said Henry, sitting on the floor. 'And I'm not going.'

Mum and Dad stuffed Henry into his pageboy
clothes. It was hard, heavy work.

Finally everyone was in the
car.

'We're going to be late!'
shrieked Mum.

'We're going to be
late!' shrieked Dad.

'We're going to be
late!' shrieked Perfect
Peter.

'Good!' muttered
Henry.

Mum, Dad, Henry and Peter
arrived at the church. Boom! There
was a clap of thunder. Rain
poured down. All the other
guests were already inside.

'Watch out for the
puddle, boys,' said
Mum, as she leapt
out of the car. She
opened her
umbrella.

Dad jumped over the puddle.

Peter jumped over the puddle.

Henry jumped over the puddle, and tripped.

SPLASH!

'Oopsy,' said Henry.

His ruffles were torn, his knickerbockers were filthy, and his satin shoes were soaked.

Mum, Dad and Peter were covered in muddy water.

Perfect Peter burst into tears.

'You've ruined my pageboy clothes,' sobbed Peter.

Mum wiped as much dirt as she could off Henry and Peter.

'It was an accident, Mum, really,' said Henry.

'Hurry up, you're late!' shouted Pimply Paul.

Mum and Dad dashed into the church. Henry and Peter stayed outside, waiting to make their entrance.

Pimply Paul and his best man, Cross Colin, stared at Henry and Peter.

'You look a mess,' said Paul.

'It was an accident,' said Henry.

Peter snivelled.

'Now be careful with the wedding rings,' said Cross Colin. He handed Henry and Peter a satin cushion each, with a gold ring on top.

A great quivering lump of lace and taffeta and bows and flowers approached. Henry guessed Prissy Polly must be lurking somewhere underneath.

'Eeek,' squeaked the clump. 'Why did it have to rain on my wedding?'

'Eeek,' squeaked the clump again. 'You're filthy.'

Perfect Peter began to sob. The satin cushion trembled in his hand. The ring balanced precariously near the edge.

89

Cross Colin snatched Peter's cushion.

'You can't carry a ring with your hand shaking like that,' snapped Colin. 'You'd better carry them both, Henry.'

'Come *on*,' hissed Pimply Paul. 'We're late!'

Cross Colin and Pimply Paul dashed into the church.

The music started. Henry pranced down the aisle after Polly. Everyone stood up.

Henry beamed and bowed and waved. He was King Henry the Horrible, smiling graciously at his cheering subjects before he chopped off their heads.

As he danced along, he stepped on Polly's long trailing dress.

Riiiip.

'Eeeeek!' squeaked Prissy Polly.

Part of Polly's train lay beneath Henry's muddy satin shoe.

That dress was too long anyway, thought Henry. He picked the fabric out of the way and stomped down the aisle.

The bride, groom, best man, and pageboys assembled in front of the vicar.

Henry stood . . . and stood . . . and stood. The vicar droned on . . . and on . . . and on. Henry's arm holding up the cushion began to ache.

This is boring, thought Henry, jiggling the rings on the cushion.

Boing! Boing! Boing!

Oooh, thought Henry. I'm good at ring tossing.

The rings bounced.

The vicar droned.

Henry was a famous pancake chef, tossing the pancakes higher and higher and higher . . .

Clink clunk.

The rings rolled down the aisle and vanished down a small grate.

Oops, thought Henry.

'May I have the rings, please?' said the minister.

Everyone looked at Henry.

'He's got them,' said Henry desperately, pointing at Peter.

'I have not,' sobbed Peter.

Henry reached into his pocket. He found two pieces of old chewing-gum, some gravel, and his lucky pirate ring.

'Here, use this,' he said.

At last, Pimply Paul and Prissy Polly were married.

Cross Colin handed Henry and Peter a basket of pink and yellow rose petals each.

'Throw the petals in front of the bride and groom

as they walk back down the aisle,' whispered Colin.

'I will,' said Peter. He scattered the petals before Pimply Paul and Prissy Polly.

'So will I,' said Henry. He hurled a handful of petals in Pimply Paul's face.

'Watch it, you little brat,' snarled Paul.

'Windy, isn't it?' said Henry. He hurled another handful of petals at Polly.

'Eeek,' squeaked Prissy Polly.

'Everyone outside for photographs,' said the photographer.

Horrid Henry loved having his picture taken. He dashed out.

'Pictures of the bride and groom first,' said the photographer.

Henry jumped in front.

Click.

Henry peeked from the side.

Click.

Henry stuck out his tongue.

Click.

Henry made horrible rude faces. **Click.**

'This way to the reception!' said Cross Colin. The wedding party was held in a nearby hotel.

The adults did nothing but talk and eat, talk and drink, talk and eat. Perfect Peter sat at the table and ate his lunch.

Horrid Henry sat under the table and poked people's legs. He crawled around and squashed some toes. Then Henry got bored and drifted into the next room.

There was the wedding cake, standing alone, on a table. It was the most delicious-looking cake Henry had ever seen. It had three layers and was covered in luscious white icing and yummy iced flowers and bells and leaves.

Henry's mouth watered.

I'll just taste a teeny weeny bit of petal, thought Henry. No harm in that.

He broke off a morsel and popped it in his mouth.

Hmmmmm boy! That icing tasted great.

Perhaps just one more bite, thought Henry. If I take it from the back, no one will notice.

Henry carefully selected an icing rose from the bottom tier and stuffed it in his mouth. Wow.

Henry stood back from the case. It looked a little uneven now, with that rose missing from the bottom.

I'll just even it up, thought Henry. It was the work of a moment to break off a rose from the middle tier and another from the top.

Then a strange thing happened.

'Eat me,' whispered the cake. 'Go on.'

Who was Henry to ignore such a request?

He picked out a few crumbs from the back.

Delicious, thought Henry. Then he took a few more. And a few more. Then he dug out a nice big chunk.

'What do you think you're doing?' shouted Pimply Paul.

Henry ran round the cake table. Paul ran after him. Round and round and round the cake they ran.

'Just wait till I get my hands on you!' snarled Pimply Paul.

Henry dashed under the table.
Pimply Paul lunged for him and missed.

SPLAT.

Pimply Paul fell head first on to the cake.
Henry slipped away.

Prissy Polly ran into the room.
'Eeek,' she shrieked.

'Wasn't that a lovely wedding,' sighed Mum on the way home. 'Funny they didn't have a cake, though.'

'Oh yes,' said Dad.

'Oh yes,' said Peter.

'OH YES!' said Henry. 'I'll be glad to be a pageboy any time.'

Dear Cousins,

Paul and I are sorry to have taken so long to send this thankyou letter for the lovely toaster you gave us, but it has taken a while to recover from our eventful wedding. When Paul fell onto the cake he hurt his nose and the bandages have only just come off.

I suppose most pageboys lose the rings and throw rose petals at the bride instead of in front of her and fall into puddles and ruin their very expensive pageboy outfits that the bride and groom have paid for and step on the bride's dress and rip it though I have yet to meet one.

As Henry managed to get himself into all of our wedding pictures, we won't be forgetting him in a hurry. If you would like any copies we would happily send you a set.

Love from your cousins,
Polly and Paul

P.S. we've enclosed Henry's pirate ring.

HORRID HENRY'S
Hike

Horrid Henry looked out of the window.
HAAARRRGGGHHH! It was a lovely day.
The sun was shining. The birds were tweeting.
The breeze was blowing. Little fluffy clouds floated by
in a bright blue sky.

Rats.

Why couldn't it be raining? Or hailing? Or
sleeting?

Any minute, any second, it would happen…the
words he'd been dreading, the words he'd give
anything not to hear, the words –

'Henry! Peter! Time to go for a walk,' called Mum.

'Yippee!' said Perfect Peter. 'I can wear my new
yellow wellies!'

'NO!' screamed Horrid Henry.

Go for a walk! Go for a walk! Didn't he walk enough already? He walked to school. He walked home from school. He walked to the TV. He walked to the computer. He walked to the sweet jar *and* all the way back to the comfy black chair. Horrid Henry walked plenty. Ugghh. The last thing he needed was more walking. More chocolate, yes. More crisps, yes. More *walking*? No way! Why oh why couldn't his parents ever say, 'Henry! Time to play on the computer.' Or 'Henry, stop doing your homework this minute! Time to turn on the TV.'

But no. For some reason his mean, horrible parents thought he spent too much time sitting indoors. They'd been threatening for weeks to make him go on a family walk. Now the dreadful moment had come. His precious weekend was ruined.

Horrid Henry hated nature. Horrid Henry hated fresh air. What could be more boring than walking up and down streets staring at lamp posts? Or sloshing across some stupid muddy park? Nature smelled. Uggh! He'd much rather be inside watching TV.

Mum stomped into the sitting room.

'Henry! Didn't you hear me calling?'

'No,' lied Henry.

'Get your wellies on, we're going,' said Dad, rubbing his hands. 'What a lovely day.'

'I don't want to go for a walk,' said Henry. 'I want to watch *Rapper Zapper Zaps Terminator Gladiator*.'

'But Henry,' said Perfect Peter, 'fresh air and exercise are so good for you.'

'I don't care!' shrieked Henry.

Horrid Henry stomped downstairs and flung open the front door. He breathed in deeply, hopped on one foot, then shut the door.

'There! Done it. Fresh air *and* exercise,' snarled Henry.

'Henry, we're going,' said Mum. 'Get in the car.'

Henry's ears pricked up.

'The car?' said Henry. 'I thought we were going for a walk.'

'We are,' said Mum. 'In the countryside.'

'Hurray!' said Perfect Peter. 'A nice *long* walk.'

'NOOOO!' howled Henry. Plodding along in the boring old park was bad enough, with its mouldy leaves and dog poo and stumpy trees. But at least the park wasn't very big. But the *countryside*?

The countryside was enormous! They'd be walking for hours, days, weeks, months, till his legs wore down to stumps and his feet fell off. And the countryside was so dangerous! Horrid Henry was sure he'd be swallowed up by quicksand or trampled to death by marauding chickens.

'I live in the city!' shrieked Henry. 'I don't want to go to the country!'

'Time you got out more,' said Dad.

'But look at those clouds,' moaned Henry, pointing to a fluffy wisp. 'We'll get soaked.'

'A little water never hurt anyone,' said Mum.

Oh yeah? Wouldn't they be sorry when he died of pneumonia.

'I'm staying here and that's final!' screamed Henry.

'Henry, we're waiting,' said Mum.

'Good,' said Henry.

'*I'm* all ready, Mum,' said Peter.

'I'm going to start deducting pocket money,' said Dad. '5p, 10p, 15p, 20— '

Horrid Henry pulled on his wellies, stomped out of the door and got in the car. He slammed the door as hard as he could. It was so unfair! Why did he never get to do what *he* wanted to do? Now he would miss the first time Rapper Zapper had ever slugged it out with Terminator Gladiator. And all because he had to go on a long, boring, exhausting, horrible hike. He was so miserable he didn't even have the energy to kick Peter.

'Can't we just walk round the block?' moaned Henry.

'N-O spells no,' said Dad. 'We're going for a lovely walk in the countryside and that's that.'

Horrid Henry slumped miserably in his seat. Boy would they be sorry when he was gobbled up by goats. Boo hoo, if only we hadn't gone on that walk in the wilds, Mum would wail. Henry was right, we should have listened to him, Dad would sob.

I miss Henry, Peter would howl. I'll never eat goat's cheese again. And now it's too late, they would shriek.

If only, thought Horrid Henry. That would serve them right.

All too soon, Mum pulled into a car park, on the edge of a small wood.

'Wow,' said Perfect Peter. 'Look at all those lovely trees.'

'Bet there are werewolves hiding there,' muttered Henry. 'And I hope they come and eat you!'

'Mum!' squealed Peter. 'Henry's trying to scare me.'

'Don't be horrid, Henry,' said Mum.

Horrid Henry looked around him. There was a gate, leading to endless meadows bordered by

hedgerows. A muddy path wound through the trees
and across the fields. A church spire stuck up in the
distance.

'Right, I've seen the countryside, let's go home,'
said Henry.

Mum glared at him.

'What?' said Henry, scowling.

'Let's enjoy this lovely day,' said Dad, sighing.

'So what do we do now?' said Henry.

'Walk,' said Dad.

'Where?' said Henry.

'Just walk,' said Mum, 'and enjoy the beautiful
scenery.'

Henry groaned.

'We're heading for the lake,' said Dad, striding off.
'I've brought bread and we can feed the ducks.'

'But *Rapper Zapper* starts in an hour!'

'Tough,' said Mum.

Mum, Dad, and Peter headed through the gate into the field. Horrid Henry trailed behind them walking as slowly as he could.

'Ahh, breathe the lovely fresh air,' said Mum.

'We should do this more often,' said Dad.

Henry sniffed.

The horrible smell of manure filled his nostrils.

'Ewww, smelly,' said Henry. 'Peter, couldn't you wait?'

'MUM!' shrieked Peter. 'Henry called me smelly.'

'Did not!'

'Did too!'

'Did not, smelly.'

'WAAAAAAAAA!' wailed Peter. 'Tell him to stop!'

'Don't be horrid, Henry!' screamed Mum. Her voice echoed. A dog walker passed her, and glared.

'Peter, would you rather run a mile, jump a stile, or eat a country pancake?' said Henry sweetly.

'Ooh,' said Peter. 'I love pancakes. And a country one must be even more delicious than a city one.'

'Ha ha,' cackled Horrid Henry, sticking out his tongue. 'Fooled you. Peter wants to eat cowpats!'

'MUM!' screamed Peter.

Henry walked.
    And walked.
        And walked.

His legs felt heavier, and heavier, and heavier.

'This field is muddy,' moaned Henry.

'I'm bored,' groaned Henry.

'My feet hurt,' whined Henry.

'Can't we go home? We've already walked miles,' whinged Henry.

'We've been walking for ten minutes,' said Dad.

'Please can we go on walks more often,' said Perfect Peter. 'Oh, look at those fluffy little sheepies!'

Horrid Henry pounced. He was a zombie biting the head off the hapless human.

'AAAAEEEEEE!' squealed Peter.

'Henry!' screamed Mum.

'Stop it!' screamed Dad. 'Or no TV for a week.'

When he was king, thought Horrid Henry, any parent who made their children go on a hike would be dumped barefoot in a scorpion-infested desert.

Plod.

Plod.

Plod.

Horrid Henry dragged his feet. Maybe his horrible mean parents would get fed up waiting for him and turn back, he thought, kicking some mouldy leaves.

Squelch.

Squelch.

Squelch.

Oh no, not *another* muddy meadow.

And then suddenly Horrid Henry had an idea. What was he thinking? All that fresh air must be rotting his brain. The sooner they got to the stupid lake, the sooner they could get home for the *Rapper Zapper Zaps Terminator Gladiator*.

'Come on, everyone, let's run!' shrieked Henry. 'Race you down the hill to the lake!'

'That's the spirit, Henry,' said Dad.

Horrid Henry dashed past Dad.

'OW!' shrieked Dad, tumbling into the stinging nettles.

Horrid Henry whizzed past Mum.

'Eww!' shrieked Mum, slipping in a cowpat.

Splat!

Horrid Henry pushed past Peter.
'Waaa!' wailed Peter. 'My wellies
are getting dirty.'
Horrid Henry scampered
down the muddy path.
'Wait Henry!' yelped Mum. 'It's
too slipp – aaaiiieeeee!'
Mum slid down
the path on her
bottom.
'Slow
down!'
puffed
Dad.

'I can't run that fast,'
wailed Peter.
But Horrid
Henry raced on.
'Shortcut
across the
field!'
he
called.

'Come on slowcoaches!'

The black and white cow grazing alone in the middle raised its head.

'Henry!' shouted Dad.

Horrid Henry kept running.

'I don't think that's a cow!' shouted Mum.

The cow lowered its head and charged.

'It's a bull!' yelped Mum and Dad. 'RUN!'

'I said it was dangerous in the countryside!' gasped Henry, as everyone clambered over the stile in the nick of time. 'Look, there's the lake!' he added, pointing.

Henry ran down to the water's edge. Peter followed. The embankment narrowed to a point. Peter slipped past Henry and bagged the best spot, right at the water's edge where the ducks gathered.

'Hey, get away from there,' said Henry.

'I want to feed the ducks,' said Peter.

'I want to feed the ducks,' said Henry. 'Now move.'

'I was here first,' said Peter.

'Not any more,' said Henry.

Horrid Henry pushed Peter.

'Out of my way, worm!'

Perfect Peter pushed him back.

'Don't call me worm!'

Henry wobbled.

Peter wobbled.

 Splash!

Peter tumbled into the lake.

 Crash!

Henry tumbled into the lake.

'My babies!' shrieked Mum, jumping in after them.

'My – glug glug glug!' shrieked Dad, jumping into the muddy water after her.

'My new wellies!' gurgled Perfect Peter.

Bang!

Pow!

Terminator Gladiator slashed at Rapper Zapper.

Zap!

Rapper Zapper slashed back.

'Go Zappy!' yelled Henry, lying bundled up in blankets on the sofa. Once everyone had scrambled out of the lake, Mum and Dad had been keen to get home as fast as possible.

'I think the park next time,' mumbled Dad, sneezing.

'Definitely,' mumbled Mum, coughing.

'Oh, I don't know,' said Horrid Henry happily. 'A little water never hurt anyone.'

Horrid Henry's Nature Guide

Beware! Danger!

Every time you step off a concrete path you are leaving civilisation! The countryside is full of dangers. You will meet:

wild beasts

dangerous paths

swollen rivers

stinging nettles

rampaging chickens

quicksand

horrible smells

mud

zombies

vampires

Beware!
Fresh air.

mummies...

Take it from me – don't leave town. Remember what happened to Hansel and Gretel! It could happen to you! Stay at home and watch TV.

HORRID HENRY Dines at Restaurant Le Posh

'G reat news, everyone,' said Mum, beaming. 'Aunt Ruby is taking us all out for dinner to Le Posh, the best French restaurant in town.'

'Oh boy, Restaurant Le Posh,' said Perfect Peter.
'We've never been there.'

Horrid Henry stopped scribbling all over Peter's
stamp album. His heart sank. French? Restaurant? Oh
no. That meant strange, horrible, yucky food. That
meant no burgers, no ketchup, no pizza. That meant –

'**NOOOOOOOOOO!** I don't want to go there!'
howled Henry. Who knew what revolting poison
would arrive on his plate, covered in gloopy sauce
with green bits floating about. **Uggghh**.

'It's Mum's birthday,' said Dad, 'so we're celebrating.'

'I only like Whopper Whoopee,' said Henry. 'Or
Fat Frank's. I don't want to go to Le Posh.'

'But Henry,' said Perfect Peter, tidying up his toys,
'it's a chance to try new food.'

Mum beamed. 'Quite right, Peter. It's always nice
to try new things.'

'No it isn't,' snarled Horrid Henry. 'I hate trying
new food when there's nothing wrong with the old.'

'I love it,' said Dad. 'I eat everything except
tomatoes.'

'And I eat everything except squid,' said Mum.

'And I love all vegetables except beetroot,' said
Perfect Peter. 'Especially spinach and sprouts.'

'Well I don't,' shrieked Horrid Henry. 'Do they
have pasta?'

'Whatever they have will be delicious,' said Mum firmly.

'Do they have burgers? If they don't I'm not going,' wailed Horrid Henry.

Mum looked at Dad.

Dad looked at Mum.

Last time they'd taken Henry to a fancy restaurant he'd had a tantrum under the table. The time before he'd run screaming round the room snatching all the salt and pepper shakers and then thrown up on the people at the next table. The time before that – Mum and Dad preferred not to think about that.

'Shall we get a babysitter?' murmured Dad.

'Leave him home on my birthday?' murmured Mum. She allowed herself to be tempted for a moment. Then she sighed.

'Henry, you are coming and you will be on your best behaviour,' said Mum. 'Your cousin Steve will be there. You wouldn't want Steve to see you make a fuss, would you?'

The hairs on the back of Henry's neck stood up. Steve! Stuck-Up Steve! Horrid Henry's arch-enemy and world's worst cousin. If there was a slimier boy than Steve slithering around then Horrid Henry would eat worms.

Last time they'd met Henry had tricked Steve into thinking there was a monster under his bed. Steve had sworn revenge. There was nothing Steve wouldn't do to get back at Henry.

Boy, did Horrid Henry hate Stuck-Up Steve.

Boy, did Stuck-Up Steve hate Horrid Henry.

'I'm not coming and that's final!' screamed Horrid Henry.

'Henry,' said Dad. 'I'll make a deal with you.'

'What deal?' said Henry. It was always wise to be suspicious when parents offered deals.

'I want you to be pleasant and talk to everyone. And you will eat everything on your plate like everyone else without making a fuss. If you do, I'll give you £2.'

£2! Two whole pounds! Horrid Henry gasped. Two whole pounds just for talking and shoving a few mouthfuls of disgusting food in his mouth. Normally he had to do that for free.

'How about £3?' said Henry.

'Henry . . .' said Mum.

'OK, deal,' said Horrid Henry. But I won't eat a thing and they can't make me, he thought. He'd find a way. Dad said he had to eat everything on his plate. Well, maybe some food wouldn't stay on his plate. . . Horrid Henry smiled.

Perfect Peter stopped putting away his bricks. He frowned. Shouldn't he get two pounds like Henry?

'What's my reward for being good?' said Perfect Peter.

'Goodness is its own reward,' said Dad.

The restaurant was hushed. The tables were covered in snowy-white tablecloths, with yellow silk chairs. Huge gold chandeliers dangled from the ceiling. Crystal glasses twinkled. The rectangular china plates sparkled. Horrid Henry was impressed.

'Wow,' said Henry. It was like walking into a palace.

'Haven't you ever been here before?' sneered Stuck-Up Steve.

'No,' said Henry.

'*We* eat here all the time,' said Steve. 'I guess you're too poor.'

'It's 'cause *we'd* rather eat at Whopper Whoopee,' lied Henry.

'Hush, Steve,' said Rich Aunt Ruby. 'I'm sure Whopper Whoopee is a lovely restaurant.'

Steve snorted.

Henry kicked him under the table.

'**OWWWW!**' yelped Steve. 'Henry kicked me!'

'No I didn't,' said Henry. 'It was an accident.'

'Henry,' said Mum through gritted teeth. 'Remember what we said about best behaviour? We're in a fancy restaurant.'

Horrid Henry scowled. He looked cautiously around. It was just as he'd feared. Everyone was busy eating weird bits of this and that, covered in gloopy sauces. Henry checked under the tables to see if anyone was being sick yet.

There was no one lying poisoned under the tables. I guess it's just a matter of time, thought Henry grimly. You won't catch me eating anything here.

Mum, Dad, Peter and Rich Aunt Ruby blabbed away at their end of the table. Horrid Henry sat sullenly next to Stuck-Up Steve.

'I've got a new bike,' Steve bragged. 'Do you still have that old rust bucket you had last Christmas?'

'Hush, Steve,' said Rich Aunt Ruby.

Horrid Henry's foot got ready to kick Steve.

'Boudicca Battle-Axe! How many times have I told you − don't chew with your mouth open,' boomed a terrible voice.

Horrid Henry looked up. His jaw dropped.

There was his terrifying teacher, Miss Battle-Axe, sitting at a small table in the corner with her back to him. She was with someone even taller, skinnier, and more ferocious than she was.

'And take your elbows off the table!'

'Yes, Mum,' said Miss Battle-Axe meekly.

Henry could not believe his ears. Did teachers have mothers? Did teachers ever leave the school? Impossible.

'Boudicca! Stop slouching!'

'Yes, Mum,' said Miss Battle-Axe, straightening up a fraction.

'So, what's everyone having?' beamed Aunt Ruby. Horrid Henry tore his eyes away from Miss Battle-Axe and stared at the menu. It was entirely written in French.

'I recommend the mussels,' said Aunt Ruby.

'Mussels! Ick!' shrieked Henry.

'Or the blah blah blah blah blah.' Aunt Ruby pronounced a few mysterious French words.

'Maybe,' said Mum. She looked a little uncertain.

'Maybe,' said Dad. He looked a little uncertain.

'You order for me, Aunt Ruby,' said Perfect Peter. 'I eat everything.'

Horrid Henry had no idea what food Aunt Ruby had suggested, but he knew he hated every single thing on the menu.

'I want a burger,' said Henry.

'No burgers here,' said Mum firmly. 'This is Restaurant Le Posh.'

'I said I want a burger!' shouted Henry. Several diners looked up.

'Don't be horrid, Henry!' hissed Mum.

'I CAN'T UNDERSTAND THIS MENU!' screamed Henry.

'Calm down this minute Henry,' hissed Dad. 'Or no £2.'

Mum translated: 'A tasty . . . uh . . . something on a bed of roast something with a something sauce.'

'Sounds delicious,' said Dad.

'Wait, there's more,' said Mum. 'A big piece of something enrobed with something cooked in something with carrots.'

'Right, I'm having that,' said Dad. 'I love carrots.'

Mum carried on translating. Henry opened his mouth to scream –

'Why don't you order *tripe*?' said Steve.

'What's that?' asked Henry suspiciously.

129

'You don't want to know,' said Steve.

'Try me,' said Henry.

'Intestines,' said Steve. 'You know, the wriggly bits in your stomach.'

Horrid Henry snorted. Sometimes he felt sorry for Steve. Did Steve really think he'd fool him with *that* old trick? *Tripe* was probably a fancy French word for spaghetti. Or trifle.

'Or you could order *escargots*,' said Steve. 'I dare you.'

'What's *escargots*?' said Henry.

Stuck-Up Steve stuck his nose in the air.

'Oh, sorry, I forgot you don't learn French at your school. *I've* been learning it for years.'

'Whoopee for you,' said Horrid Henry.

'*Escargots* are snails, stupid,' said Stuck-Up Steve.

Steve must think he was a real idiot, thought Horrid Henry indignantly. *Snails*. Ha ha ha. In a restaurant? As if.

'Oh yeah, right, you big fat liar,' said Henry.

Steve shrugged.

'Too chicken, huh?' he sneered. 'Cluck cluck cluck.'

Horrid Henry was outraged. No one called him chicken and lived.

'Course not,' said Horrid Henry. 'I'd love to eat snails.' Naturally it would turn out to be fish or something in a smelly, disgusting sauce, but so what? *Escargots* could hardly be more revolting than all the other yucky things on the menu. Steve would have to try harder than that to fool him. He would order so-called 'snails' just to show Steve up for the liar he was. Then wouldn't he make fun of stupid old Steve!

'And vat are ve having tonight?' asked the French waiter.

Aunt Ruby ordered.

'An excellent choice, madame,' said the waiter.

Dad ordered. The waiter kissed his fingers.

'*Magnifique*, monsieur, our speciality.'

Mum ordered.

'Bravo, madame. And what about you, young man?' the waiter asked Henry.

'I'm having *escargots*,' said Henry.

'Hmmn,' said the waiter. 'Monsieur is a gourmet?'

Horrid Henry wasn't sure he liked the sound of that. Stuck-Up Steve snickered. What was going on? thought Horrid Henry.

'Boudicca! Eat your vegetables!'

'Yes, Mum.'

'Boudicca! Stop slurping.'

'Yes, Mum,' snapped Miss Battle-Axe.

'Boudicca! Don't pick your nose!'

'I wasn't!' said Miss Battle-Axe.

'Don't you contradict me,' said Mrs Battle-Axe.

The waiter reappeared, carrying six plates covered in silver domes.

'Voilà!' he said, whisking off the lids with a flourish. '*Bon appétit!*'

Everyone peered at their elegant plates.

'Ah,' said Mum, looking at her squid.

'Ah,' said Dad, looking at his stuffed tomatoes.

'Ah,' said Peter, looking at his beetroot mousse.

Horrid Henry stared at his food. It looked like –

it couldn't be − oh my God, it was . . . SNAILS! It
really was snails! Squishy squashy squidgy slimy
slithery slippery snails. Still in their shells. Drenched
in butter, but unmistakably snails. Steve had tricked
him.

Horrid Henry's hand reached out to hurl the snails
at Steve.

Stuck-Up Steve giggled.

Horrid Henry stopped and gritted his teeth. No
way was he giving Steve the satisfaction of seeing him
get into big trouble. He'd ordered snails and he'd eat
snails. And when he threw up, he'd make sure it was
all over Steve.

Horrid Henry grabbed his fork and plunged. Then
he closed his eyes and popped the snail in his mouth.

Horrid Henry chewed.

Horrid Henry chewed some more.

'Hmmn,' said Horrid Henry.

He popped another snail in
his mouth. And another.

'Yummy,' said Henry. 'This is
brilliant.' Why hadn't anyone told
him that Le Posh served such
thrillingly revolting food? Wait till
he told Rude Ralph!

Stuck-Up Steve looked unhappy.

'How's your maggot sauce,
Steve?' said Henry cheerfully.

'It's not maggot sauce,' said Steve.

'Maggot maggot maggot,'
whispered Henry. 'Watch them
wriggle about.'

Steve put down his fork. So did
Mum, Dad, and Peter.

'Go on everyone, eat up,' said Henry,
chomping.

'I'm not that hungry,' said Mum.

'You said we had to eat everything on our plate,'
said Henry.

'No I didn't,' said Dad weakly.

'You did too!' said Henry. 'So eat!'

'I don't like beetroot,' moaned Perfect Peter.

'Hush, Peter,' snapped Mum.

'Peter, I never thought *you* were a fussy eater,' said Aunt Ruby.

'I'm not!' wailed Perfect Peter.

'Boudicca!' blasted Mrs Battle-Axe's shrill voice. 'Pay attention when I'm speaking to you!'

'Yes, Mum,' said Miss Battle-Axe.

'Why can't you be as good as that boy?' said Mrs Battle-Axe, pointing to Horrid Henry. 'Look at him sitting there, eating so beautifully.'

Miss Battle-Axe turned round and saw Henry. Her face went bright red, then purple, then white. She gave him a sickly smile.

Horrid Henry gave her a little polite wave. Oh boy.

For the first time in his life was he ever looking forward to school.

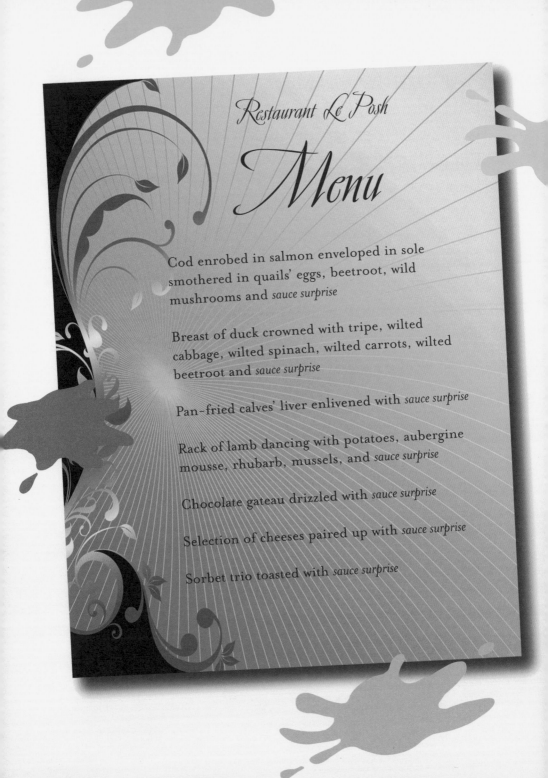

Restaurant Le Posh

Menu

Cod enrobed in salmon enveloped in sole smothered in quails' eggs, beetroot, wild mushrooms and *sauce surprise*

Breast of duck crowned with tripe, wilted cabbage, wilted spinach, wilted carrots, wilted beetroot and *sauce surprise*

Pan-fried calves' liver enlivened with *sauce surprise*

Rack of lamb dancing with potatoes, aubergine mousse, rhubarb, mussels, and *sauce surprise*

Chocolate gateau drizzled with *sauce surprise*

Selection of cheeses paired up with *sauce surprise*

Sorbet trio toasted with *sauce surprise*

HORRiD HENRY'S
Ambush

It was Christmas Eve at last. Every minute felt like an hour. Every hour felt like a year. How could Henry live until Christmas morning when he could get his hands on all his loot?

Mum and Dad were baking frantically in the kitchen.

Perfect Peter sat by the twinkling Christmas tree scratching out 'Silent Night' over and over again on his cello.

'Can't you play something else?' snapped Henry.

'No,' said Peter, sawing away. 'This is the only Christmas carol I know. You can move if you don't like it.'

'You move,' said Henry.

Peter ignored him.

'Siiiiiiiii—lent Niiiiight,' screeched the cello.

AAARRRGH.

Horrid Henry lay on the sofa with his fingers in his ears, double-checking his choices from the Toy Heaven catalogue. Big red 'X's' appeared on every page, to help you-know-who remember all the toys he absolutely had to have. Oh please, let everything he wanted leap from its pages and into Santa's sack. After all, what could be better than looking at a huge glittering stack of presents on Christmas morning, and knowing that they were all for you?

Oh please let this be the year when he finally got everything he wanted!

His letter to Father Christmas couldn't have been clearer.

139

Dear Father Christmas

I want loads and loads of cash,
to make up for the puny ammount you
put in my stocking last year. And a
Robomatic Supersonic Space Howler Deluxe
plus attachments would be great, too.
I have asked for this before, you know!
And the Terminator Gladiator fighting
kit. I need lots more Day-Glo Slime
and comics and a Mutant Max
poster and the new Zapatron HipHop
Dinosaur. This is your last chance.

Henry

P.S. Satsumas are NOT presents!!!

P.P.S Peter asked me to tell you to
give me all his presents as
he doesn't want any.

140

How hard could it be for Father Christmas to get this right? He'd asked for the Space Howler last year, and it never arrived. Instead, Henry got . . . vests. And handkerchiefs. And books. And clothes. And a – **blecccccch** – jigsaw puzzle and a skipping rope and a tiny supersoaker instead of the mega-sized one he'd specified. Yuck! Father Christmas obviously needed Henry's help.

Father Christmas is getting old and doddery, thought Henry. Maybe he hasn't got my letters. Maybe he's lost his reading glasses. Or – what a horrible thought – maybe he was delivering Henry's presents by mistake to some other Henry. Eeeek! Some yucky, undeserving Henry was probably right now this minute playing with Henry's Terminator Gladiator sword, shield, axe, and trident. And enjoying his Intergalactic Samurai Gorillas. It was so unfair!

And then suddenly Henry had a brilliant, spectacular idea. Why had he never thought of this before? All his present problems would be over.

Presents were far too important to leave to Father Christmas. Since he couldn't be trusted to bring the right gifts, Horrid Henry had no choice. He would have to ambush Father Christmas.

Yes!

He'd hold Father Christmas hostage with his Goo-Shooter, while he rummaged in his present sack for all the loot he was owed. Maybe Henry would keep the lot. Now *that* would be fair.

Let's see, thought Horrid Henry. Father Christmas was bound to be a slippery character, so he'd need to booby-trap his bedroom. When you-know-who sneaked in to fill his stocking at the end of the bed, Henry could leap up and nab him. Father Christmas had a lot of explaining to do for all those years of stockings filled with satsumas and walnuts instead of chocolate and cold hard cash.

So, how best to capture him?

Henry considered.

A bucket of water above the door.

A skipping rope stretched tight across the entrance, guaranteed to trip up intruders.

A web of string criss-crossed from bedpost to door and threaded with bells to ensnare night-time visitors.

And let's not forget strategically scattered whoopee cushions.

His plan was foolproof.

Loot, here I come, thought Horrid Henry.

Horrid Henry sat up in bed, his Goo-Shooter aimed at the half-open door where a bucket of water balanced. All his traps were laid. No one was getting in without Henry knowing about it. Any minute now, he'd catch Father Christmas and make him pay up.

Henry waited. And waited. And waited. His eyes started to feel heavy and he closed them for a moment.

There was a rustling at Henry's door.

Oh my god, this was it! Henry lay down and pretended to be asleep.

Cr-eeeek.

       Cr-eeeek.

Horrid Henry reached for his Goo-Shooter.

A huge shape loomed in the doorway.

Henry braced himself to attack.

'Doesn't he look sweet when he's asleep?' whispered the shape.

'What a little snugglechops,' whispered another.

Sweet? Snugglechops?

Horrid Henry's fingers itched to let Mum and Dad have it with both barrels. **Pow! Splat!**

Henry could see it now. Mum covered in green goo. Dad covered in green goo. Mum and Dad snatching the Goo-Shooter and wrecking all his plans and throwing out all his presents and banning him from TV for ever . . . hmmmn. His fingers felt a little less itchy.

Henry lowered his Goo-Shooter. The bucket of water wobbled above the door.

Yikes! What if Mum and Dad stepped into his Santa traps? All his hard work – ruined.

'I'm awake,' snarled Henry.

The shapes stepped back. The water stopped wobbling.

'Go to sleep!' hissed Mum.

'Go to sleep!' hissed Dad.

'What are you doing here?' demanded Henry.

'Checking on you,' said Mum. 'Now go to sleep or Father Christmas will never come.'

He'd better, thought Henry.

Horrid Henry woke with a jolt.

AAARRGGH! He'd fallen asleep. How could he? Panting and gasping Henry switched on the light. Phew. His traps were intact. His stocking was empty. Father Christmas hadn't been yet.

Wow, was that lucky. That was incredibly lucky. Henry lay back, his heart pounding. And then Horrid Henry had a terrible thought.

What if Father Christmas had decided to be spiteful and *avoid* Henry's bedroom this year? Or what if he'd played a sneaky trick on Henry and filled a stocking *downstairs* instead?

Nah. No way.

But wait. When Father Christmas came to Rude Ralph's house he always filled the stockings downstairs. Now Henry came to think of it, Moody

Margaret always left her stocking downstairs too, hanging from the fireplace, not from the end of her bed, like Henry did.

Horrid Henry looked at the clock. It was past midnight. Mum and Dad had forbidden him to go downstairs till morning, on pain of having all his presents taken away and no telly all day.

But this was an emergency. He'd creep downstairs, take a quick peek to make sure he hadn't missed Father Christmas, then be back in bed in a jiffy.

No one will ever know, thought Horrid Henry.

Henry tiptoed round the whoopee cushions, leaped over the criss-cross threads, stepped over the skipping rope and carefully squeezed through his door so as not to disturb the bucket of water. Then he crept downstairs.

Sneak
Sneak
Sneak

Horrid Henry shone his torch over the sitting room. Father Christmas hadn't been. The room was exactly as he'd left it that evening.

Except for one thing. Henry's light illuminated the Christmas tree, heavy with chocolate santas and chocolate bells and chocolate reindeer. Mum and Dad must have hung them on the tree after he'd gone to bed.

147

Horrid Henry looked at the chocolates cluttering up the Christmas tree. Shame, thought Horrid Henry, the way those chocolates spoil the view of all those lovely decorations. You could barely see the baubles and tinsel he and Peter had worked so hard to put on.

'Hi, Henry,' said the chocolate santas. 'Don't you want to eat us?'

'Go on, Henry,' said the chocolate bells. 'You know you want to.'

'What are you waiting for, Henry?' urged the chocolate reindeer.

What indeed? After all, it *was* Christmas.

Henry took a chocolate santa or three from the side, and then another two from the back. Hmmn, boy, was that great chocolate, he thought, stuffing them into his mouth.

Oops. Now the chocolate santas looked a little unbalanced.

Better take a few from the front and from the other side, to even it up, thought Henry. Then no one will notice there are a few chocolates missing.

Henry gobbled and gorged and guzzled. Wow, were those chocolates yummy!!!

The tree looks a bit bare,
thought Henry a little while later.
Mum had such eagle eyes she
might notice that a few — well,
all — of the chocolates were
missing. He'd better hide all
those gaps with a few extra
baubles. And, while he was
improving the tree, he could
swap that stupid fairy for
Terminator Gladiator.

Henry piled extra
decorations onto the branches.
Soon the Christmas tree was so
covered in baubles and tinsel there
was barely a hint of
green. No one would notice the
missing chocolates. Then
Henry stood on a chair,
dumped the fairy, and,
standing on his
tippy-tippy toes,
hung Terminator
Gladiator at the
top where he
belonged.

Perfect, thought Horrid Henry, jumping off the chair and stepping back to admire his work. Absolutely perfect. Thanks to me this is the best tree ever.

There was a terrible creaking sound. Then another. Then suddenly . . .

CRASH!

The Christmas tree toppled over.

Horrid Henry's heart stopped.

Upstairs he could hear Mum and Dad stirring.

'Oy! Who's down there?' shouted Dad.

RUN!!! thought Horrid Henry. Run for your life!!

Horrid Henry ran like he had never run before, up the stairs to his room before Mum and Dad could catch him. Oh please let him get there in time. His parents' bedroom door opened just as Henry dashed inside his room. He'd made it. He was safe.

Splash! The bucket of water spilled all over him.

Trip! Horrid Henry fell over the skipping rope.

Crash! Smash! Ring! Ring! jangled the bells.

PLLLLLLL! belched the whoopee cushions.

'What is going on in here?' shrieked Mum, glaring.

'Nothing,' said Horrid Henry, as he lay sprawled on the floor soaking wet and tangled up in threads and wires and rope. 'I heard a noise downstairs so I got up to check,' he added innocently.

'Tree's fallen over,' called Dad. 'Must have been overloaded. Don't worry, I'll sort it.'

'Get back to bed, Henry,' said Mum wearily. 'And don't touch your stocking till morning.'

Henry looked. And gasped. His stocking was stuffed and bulging. That mean old sneak, thought Horrid Henry indignantly. How did he do it? How had he escaped the traps?

Watch out Father Christmas, thought Horrid Henry. I'll get you next year.

Santa traps

DON'T LET SANTA GET AWAY –
HOLD HIM HOSTAGE TO MAKE
SURE YOU GET THE GIFTS
YOU DESERVE.

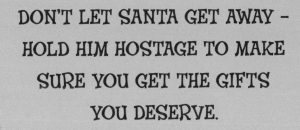

1. Hold him hostage with your Goo-Shooter or Super-Soaker so you can go through his present sack to find all those presents he keeps forgetting to give you.

2. Booby-trap the area in front of the fireplace where the stockings are hung and nab him.

3. Scatter whoopee cushions by the chimney so he can't sneak past you.

4. Whatever you do, don't block the chimney! Let Santa in first, then nab him.

HORRID HENRY'S
Rainy Day

orrid Henry was bored. Horrid Henry was fed up. He'd been banned from the computer for rampaging through Our Town Museum. He'd been banned from watching TV just because he was caught watching a *teeny* tiny bit extra after he'd been told to switch it off straight after Mutant Max. Could he help it if an exciting new series about a rebel robot had started right after? How would he know if it were any good unless he watched some of it?

It was completely unfair and all Peter's fault for telling on him, and Mum and Dad were the meanest, most horrible parents in the world.

And now he was stuck indoors, all day long, with absolutely nothing to do.

The rain splattered down. The house was grey. The world was grey. The universe was grey.

'I'm bored!' wailed Horrid Henry.

'Read a book,' said Mum.

'Do your homework,' said Dad.

'NO!' said Horrid Henry.

'Then tidy your room,' said Mum.

'Unload the dishwasher,' said Dad.

'Empty the bins,' said Mum.

'NO WAY!' shrieked Horrid Henry. What was he, a slave? Better keep out of his parents' way, or they'd come up with even more horrible things for him to do.

Horrid Henry stomped up to his boring bedroom and slammed the door. Uggh. He hated all his toys. He hated all his music. He hated all his games. **UGGGHHHHHH!** What could he do?

Aha.

He could always check to see what Peter was up to.

Perfect Peter was sitting in his room arranging stamps in his stamp album.

'Peter is a baby, Peter is a baby,' jeered Horrid Henry, sticking his head round the door.

'Don't call me baby,' said Perfect Peter.

'OK, Duke of Poop,' said Henry.

157

'Don't call me Duke!' shrieked Peter.

'OK, Poopsicle,' said Henry.

'MUUUUM!' wailed Peter. 'Henry called me Poopsicle!'

'Don't be horrid, Henry!' shouted Mum. 'Stop calling your brother names.'

Horrid Henry smiled sweetly at Peter.

'OK, Peter, 'cause I'm so nice, I'll let you make a list of ten names that you don't want to be called,' said Henry. 'And it will only cost you £1.'

£1! Perfect Peter could not believe his ears. Peter would pay much more than that never to be called Poopsicle again.

'Is this a trick, Henry?' said Peter.

'No,' said Henry. 'How dare you? I make you a good offer, and you accuse me. Well, just for that—'

'Wait,' said Peter. 'I accept.' He handed Henry a pound coin. At last, all those horrid names would be banned. Henry would never call him Duke of Poop again.

Peter got out a piece of paper and a pencil.

Now, let's see, what to put on the list, thought Peter. Poopsicle, for a start. And I hate being called Baby, and Nappy Face, and Duke of Poop. Peter wrote and wrote and wrote.

'OK, Henry, here's the list,' said Peter.

NAMES I DON'T WANT
TO BE CALLED

1. Poopsicle
2. Duke of Poop
3. Ugly
4. Nappy face
5. Baby
6 Toad
7. Smelly toad
8. Ugg
9. Worm
10. Wibble pants

Horrid Henry scanned the list. 'Fine, pongy pants,' said Henry. 'Sorry, I meant poopy pants. Or was it smelly nappy?'

'MUUUMM!' wailed Peter. 'Henry's calling me names!'

'Henry!' screamed Mum. 'For the last time, can't you leave your brother alone?'

Horrid Henry considered. *Could* he leave that worm alone?

'Peter is a frog, Peter is a frog,' chanted Henry.

'MUUUUUUMMMMM!' screamed Peter.

'That's it, Henry!' shouted Mum. 'No pocket money for a week. Go to your room and stay there.'

'Fine!' shrieked Henry. 'You'll all be sorry when I'm dead.' He stomped down the hall and slammed his bedroom door as hard as he could. *Why* were his parents so mean and horrible? He was hardly bothering Peter at all. Peter *was* a frog. Henry was only telling the truth.

Boy would they be sorry when he'd died of boredom stuck up here.

If only we'd let him watch a little extra TV, Mum would wail. Would that have been so terrible?

If only we hadn't made him do any chores, Dad would sob.

Why didn't I let Henry call me names, Peter would howl. After all, I do have smelly pants.

And now it's too late and we're sooooooo sorry, they would shriek.

But wait. *Would* they be sorry? Peter would grab his room. And all his best toys. His arch-enemy Stuck-Up Steve could come over and snatch anything he wanted, even his skeleton bank and Goo-Shooter. Peter could invade the Purple Hand fort and Henry couldn't stop him. Moody Margaret could hop over the wall and nick his flag. And his biscuits. And his Dungeon Drink Kit. Even his . . . Supersoaker.

NOOOOOO!!!

Horrid Henry went pale. He had to stop those rapacious thieves.

But how?

I could come back and haunt them, thought Horrid Henry. Yes! That would teach those grave-robbers not to mess with me.

'OOooooo, get out of my roooooooooooom, you horrrrrrrible toooooooooooooad,' he would moan at Peter.

'Touch my Goooooooooo-Shoooooter and you'll be morphed into ectoplasm,' he'd groan spookily from under Stuck-Up Steve's bed. Ha! That would show him.

Or he'd pop out from inside Moody Margaret's wardrobe.

'Giiiiive Henrrrrry's toyyyys back, you mis-er-a-ble sliiiiiimy snake,' he would rasp. That would teach her a thing or two.

Henry smiled. But fun as it would be to haunt people, he'd rather stop horrible enemies snatching his stuff in the first place.

And then suddenly Horrid Henry had a brilliant, spectacular idea. Hadn't Mum told him just the other day that people wrote wills to say who they wanted to get all their stuff when they died? Henry had been thrilled.

'So when you die I get all your money!' Henry beamed. Wow. The house would be his! And the car! And he'd be boss of the TV, 'cause it would be his, too!!! And the only shame was—

'Couldn't you just give it all to me now?' asked Henry.

'Henry!' snapped Mum. 'Don't be horrid.'

There was no time to lose. He had to write a will immediately.

Horrid Henry sat down at his desk and grabbed some paper.

MY WILL

WARNING: DO NOT READ UNLESS
I AM DEAD!!!! I mean it!!!!

If you're reading this it's because I'm dead and you aren't. I wish you were dead and I wasn't, so I could have all your stuff. It's so not fair.

First of all, to anyone thinking of snatching my stuff just 'cause I'm dead ... BEWARE! Anyone who doesn't do what I say will get haunted by a bloodless and boneless ghoul, namely me. So there.

Now the hard bit, thought Horrid Henry. Who should get his things? Was anyone deserving enough?

Peter, you are a worm. And a toad. And an ugly baby nappy face smelly ugg wibble pants poopsicle. I leave you ...hmmmn. That toad really shouldn't get anything. But Peter was his brother after all. I leave you my sweet wrappers. And a muddy twig.

That was more than Peter deserved. Still . . .

Steve, you are stuck-up and horrible and the world's worst cousin. You can have a pair of my socks. You can choose the blue ones with the holes or the falling down orange ones.

Margaret, you nit-face. I give you the Purple Hand flag to remember me by—NOT! You can have two radishes and the knight with the chopped-off head. And keep your paws off my Grisly Grub Box!!! Or else . . .

Miss Battle-Axe, you are my worst teacher ever. I leave you a broken pencil.

Aunt Ruby, you can have the lime green cardigan back that you gave me for Christmas.

Hmmm. So far he wasn't doing so well giving away any of his good things.

> Ralph, you can have my Goo-Shooter, but ONLY if you give me your football and your bike and your computer game Slime Ghouls.

That was more like it. After all, why should he be the only one writing a will? It was certainly a lot more fun thinking about *getting* stuff from other people than giving away his own treasures.

In fact, wouldn't he be better off helping others by telling them what he wanted? Wouldn't it be awful if Rich Aunt Ruby left him some of Steve's old clothes in her will thinking that he would be delighted? Better write to her at once.

Now, Steve. Henry was leaving him an old pair of holey socks. But Steve didn't have to *know* that, did he. For all Henry knew, Steve *loved* holey socks.

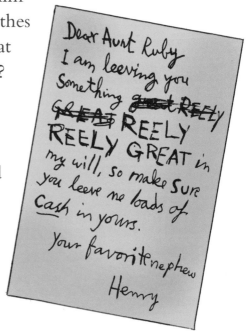

Dear Aunt Ruby
I am leeving you something ~~great REELY~~ ~~GREAT~~ REELY REELY GREAT in my will, so make sure you leeve me loads of <u>cash</u> in yours.
Your favorite nephew
Henry

> Dear Steve
>
> You know your new
> blue racing bike
> with the silver trim?
>
> Well when your dead
> it wont be any use to you,
> So please leave it to me
> in your will
>
> Your favourite cousin
> Henry
>
> P.S. By the way,
> no need to wait till your dead,
> You can give it to me now.

Right, Mum and Dad.
When they were in the
old people's home they'd
hardly need a thing.
A rocking chair and
blanket each would
do fine for them.
So, how would
Dad's music system
look in his bedroom?
And where could he
put Mum's clock radio?
Henry had always liked the chiming clock
on their mantelpiece and the picture of the blackbird.
Better go and check to see where he could put them.

167

Henry went into Mum and Dad's room, and grabbed an armload of stuff. He staggered to his bedroom and dumped everything on the floor, then went back for a second helping.

Stumbling and staggering under his heavy burden, Horrid Henry swayed down the hall and crashed into Dad.

'What are you doing?' said Dad, staring. 'That's mine.'

'And those are mine,' said Mum.

'What is going on?' shrieked Mum and Dad.

'I was just checking how all this stuff will look in my room when you're in the old people's home,' said Horrid Henry.

'I'm not there yet,' said Mum.

'Put everything back,' said Dad.

Horrid Henry scowled. Here he was, just trying to think ahead, and he gets told off.

'Well, just for that I won't leave you any of my knights in my will,' said Henry.

Honestly, some people were so selfish.

Dear Mum and Dad
Make sure you leave me all
your money in your will
(Peter says he doesn't want any).

Love from your favourite son

Henry

P.S. Don't forget to make your
will as soon as possible

Dear Great-Aunt Greta

Since you are really really old
and don't need anything,
Why not give all your money
to me?

Love from your very very poor
nephew

Henry

Margaret
You have been mean and horrid
to me for years. Why not say you're
sorry by leaving me all your
pirate hats and eye patches
and cutlasses and snickersnees
in your will? In fact, no need
to wait until you're dead - you
can say sorry by giving them all
to me RIGHT NOW!

Henry

PERFECT PETER'S
Pirate Party

'Now, let's see,' said Mum, consulting her list, 'we need pirate flags, pieces of eight, swords, treasure chests, eyepatches, skull and crossbones plates. Have I missed anything?'

Horrid Henry stopped chewing. Wow! For once, Mum was talking about something important. His Purple Hand Pirate party wasn't till next month, but it was never too soon to start getting in supplies for the birthday party of the year. No, the century.

But wait. Mum had forgotten cutlasses. They were essential for the gigantic pirate battle Henry was planning. And what about all the ketchup for fake blood? And where were the buckets of sweets?

Horrid Henry opened his mouth to speak.

'That sounds great, Mum,' piped Perfect Peter. 'But don't forget the pirate napkins.'

'Napkins. Check,' said Mum, smiling.

Huh?

'I don't want napkins at my party,' said Horrid Henry.

'This isn't for your party,' said Mum. 'It's for Peter's.'

WHAT???

'What do you mean, it's for Peter's?' gasped Horrid Henry. He felt as if an icy hand had gripped him by the throat. He was having trouble breathing.

'Peter's birthday is next week, and he's having a pirate party,' said Mum.

Perfect Peter kept eating his muesli.

'But he's having a Sammy the Snail party,' said Horrid Henry, glaring at Peter.

'I changed my mind,' said Perfect Peter.

'But pirates was *my* party idea!' shrieked Horrid Henry. 'I've been planning it for months. You're just a copycat.'

'You don't own pirates,' said Peter. 'Gordon had a pirate party for *his* birthday. So I want pirates for mine.'

'Henry, you can still have a pirate party,' said Dad.

'NOOOOOO!' screamed Horrid Henry. He couldn't have a pirate party *after* Peter. Everyone would think he'd copied his wormy toad brother.

Henry pounced. He was a poisoned arrow whizzing towards its target.

THUD! Peter fell off his chair.

SMASH! Peter's muesli bowl crashed to the floor.

'**AAAEEEIIIII!**' screeched Perfect Peter.

'Look what you've done, you horrid boy!' yelled Mum. 'Say sorry to Peter.'

'**WAAAAAAAAAA!**' sobbed Peter.

'I won't!' said Horrid Henry. 'I'm not sorry. He stole my party idea, and I hate him.'

'Then go to your room and stay there,' said Dad.

'It's not fair!' wailed Horrid Henry.

❧

'What shall we do with the drunken sailor? What shall we do with the drunken sailor?' sang Perfect Peter as he walked past Henry's slammed bedroom door.

'Make him walk the plank!' screamed Horrid Henry. 'Which is what will happen to you if you don't SHUT UP!'

'Muum! Henry told me to shut up,' yelled Peter.

'Henry! Leave your brother alone,' said Mum.

'You're the eldest. Can't you be grown-up for once and let him have his party in peace?' said Dad.

NO! thought Horrid Henry. He could not. He had to stop Peter having a pirate party. He just had to.

But how?

He could bribe Peter. But that would cost money that Henry didn't have. He could promise to be nice to him . . . No way. That was going too far. That little copycat worm did not deserve Henry's niceness.

Maybe he could *trick* him into abandoning his party idea. Hmmmm. Henry smiled. Hmmmmm.

Horrid Henry opened Peter's bedroom door and sauntered in. Perfect Peter was busy writing names on his YO HO HO pirate invitations. The same ones, Henry noticed, that *he'd* been planning to send, with the peg-legged pirate swirling his cutlass and looking like he was about to leap out at you.

'You're supposed to be in your room,' said Peter. 'I'm telling on you.'

'You know, Peter, I'm glad you're having a pirate party,' said Henry.

Peter paused.

'You are?' said Peter cautiously.

'Yeah,' said Horrid Henry. 'It means you'll get the pirate cannibal curse and I won't.'

'There's no such thing as a pirate cannibal curse,' said Peter.

'Fine,' said Horrid Henry. 'Just don't blame me when you end up as a shrunken head dangling round a cannibal's neck.'

Henry's such a liar, thought Peter. He's just trying to scare me.

'Gordon had a pirate party, and *he* didn't turn into a shrunken head,' said Peter.

Henry sighed.

'Of course not, because his name doesn't start with P. The cannibal pirate who made the curse was named Blood Boil Bob. Look, that's him on the invitations,' said Henry.

Peter glanced at the pirate. Was it his imagination, or did Blood Boil Bob have an especially mean and hungry look? Peter put down his crayon.

'He had a hateful younger brother named Paul, who became Blood Boil Bob's first shrunken head,' said Henry. 'Since then, the cannibal curse has passed down to anyone else whose name starts with P.'

'I don't believe you, Henry,' said Peter. He was sure Henry was trying to trick him. Lots of his friends had had pirate parties, and none of them had turned into a shrunken head.

On the other hand, none of his friends had names that began with P.

'How does the curse happen?' said Peter slowly.

Horrid Henry looked around. Then, putting a finger to his lips, he crept over to Peter's wardrobe and flung it open. Peter jumped.

'Just checking Blood Boil Bob's not in there,' whispered Henry. 'Now keep your voice down. Remember, dressing up as pirates, singing pirate songs, talking about treasure, wakes up the pirate cannibal. Sometimes – if you're lucky – he just steals all the

treasure. Other times he . . . POUNCES,' shrieked
Henry.

Peter turned pale.

'Yo ho, yo ho, a pirate's life for me,' sang Horrid
Henry. 'Yo ho — whoops, sorry, better not sing, in
case *he* turns up.'

'MUUUMMM!' wailed Peter. 'Henry's trying to
scare me!'

'What's
going on?'
said Mum.

'Henry
said I'm
going to turn
into a
shrunken
head if I have
a pirate party.'

'Henry, don't
be horrid,' said Mum, glaring. 'Peter, there's no such
thing.'

'Told you, Henry,' said Perfect Peter.

'If I were you I'd have a Sammy the Slug party,'
said Horrid Henry.

'Sammy the *Snail*,' said Peter. 'I'm having a pirate
party and you can't stop me. So there.'

Rats, thought Horrid Henry. How could he make Peter change his mind?

'Don't **dooooooo** **it**, Peter,' Henry howled spookily under Peter's door every night. 'Beware! Beware!'

'Stop it, Henry!' screamed Peter.

'You'll be sorry,' Horrid Henry scrawled all over Peter's homework.

'Remember the cannibal curse,' Henry whispered over supper the night before the party.

'Henry, leave your brother alone or you won't be coming to the party,' said Mum.

What? Miss out on chocolate pieces of eight? Henry scowled. That was the least he was owed.

It was so unfair. Why did Peter have to wreck everything?

It was Peter's birthday party. Mum and Dad hung two huge skull and crossbones pirate flags outside the house. The exact ones, Horrid Henry noted bitterly, that he had planned for *his* birthday party. The cutlasses had been decorated and the galleon cake eaten. All that remained was for Peter's horrible guests, Tidy Ted, Spotless Sam, Goody-Goody Gordon, Perky Parveen, Helpful Hari, Tell-Tale Tim and Mini Minnie to go on the treasure hunt.

'Yo ho, yo ho, a pirate's life for me,' sang Horrid Henry. He was wearing his pirate skull scarf, his eyepatch, and his huge black skull and crossbones hat. His bloody cutlass gleamed.

'Don't sing that,' said Peter.

'Why not, baby?' said Henry.

'You know why,' muttered Peter.

'I warned you about Blood Boil Bob, but you wouldn't listen,' hissed Henry, 'and now—' he drew his hand across his throat. 'Hey everyone, let's play pin the tail on Peter.'

'MUUUUUUUUMMMMMM!' wailed Peter.

'Behave yourself, Henry,' muttered Mum, 'or you won't be coming on the treasure hunt.'

Henry scowled. The only reason he was even at this baby party was because the treasure chest was filled with chocolate pieces of eight.

Mum clapped her hands.

'Come on everyone, look for the clues hidden around the house to help you find the pirate treasure,' she said, handing Peter a scroll. 'Here's the first one.'

Climb the stair,
if you dare,
you'll find a clue,
just for you.

'I found a clue,' squealed Helpful Hari, grabbing the scroll dangling from the banister.

Turn to the left,
turn to the right,
reach into the bag,
don't get a fright.

The party pounded off to the left, then to the right, where another scroll hung in a pouch from Peter's doorknob.

'I found the treasure map!' shouted Perky Parveen.

'Oh goody,' said Goody-Goody Gordon. Everyone gathered round the ancient scroll.

'It says to go to the park,' squealed Spotless Sam. 'Look, X marks the spot where the treasure is buried.'

Dad, waving a skull and crossbones flag, led the pirates out of the door and down the road to the park.

Horrid Henry ran ahead through the park gates and took off his skull and crossbones hat and eyepatch. No way did he want anyone to think he was part of this *baby* pirate party. He glanced at the swings. Was there anyone here that he knew? Phew, no one, just some little girl on the slide.

The little girl looked up and stared at Horrid Henry. Horrid Henry stared back.

Uh oh.

Oh no.

Henry began to back away. But it was too late.

'Henwy!' squealed the little girl. 'Henwy!'

It was Lisping Lily, New Nick's horrible sister. Henry had met her on the world's worst sleepover at Nick's house, where she—where she—

'Henwy! I love you, Henwy!' squealed Lisping Lily, running towards him. 'Will you marry with me, Henwy?'

Horrid Henry turned and ran down the windy path into the gardens. Lisping Lily ran after him. 'Henwy! Henwy!'

Henry dived into some thick bushes and crouched behind them.

Please don't find me, please don't find me, he prayed.

Henry waited, his heart pounding. All he could hear was Peter's pirate party, advancing his way. Had he lost her?

'I think the treasure's over there!' shouted Peter.

Phew. He'd ditched her. He was safe.

'Henwy?' came a little voice. 'Henwy! Where are you? I want to give you a big kiss.'

AAAARRGGHH!

Then Horrid Henry remembered who he was. The boy who'd got Miss Battle-Axe sent to the head. The boy who'd defeated the demon dinner lady. The boy who was scared of nothing (except injections). What was a pirate king like him doing hiding from some tiddly toddler?

Horrid Henry put on his pirate hat and grabbed his cutlass. He'd scare her off if it was the last thing he did.

'AAAAARRRRRRRRRRR!' roared the pirate king, leaping up and brandishing his bloody cutlass.

'AAAAAAAAAHHH!' squealed Lisping Lily. She turned and ran, crashing into Peter.

'Piwates! Piwates!' she screamed, dashing away.

Perfect Peter's blood ran cold. He looked into the thrashing bushes and saw a skull and crossbones rising out of the hedge, the gleam of sunlight on a blood-red cutlass…

'AAAAAAAHHHHHH!' screamed Peter. 'It's Blood Boil Bob!' He turned and ran.

'AAAAAAAHHHHHH!' shrieked Ted. He turned and ran.

'AAAAAAAHHHHHH!' shrieked Gordon, Parveen, and the rest. They turned and ran.

Huh? thought Horrid Henry, trying to wriggle free.

Thud!

Henry's foot knocked against something hard. There, hidden beneath some leaves under the hedge, was a pirate chest.

Eureka!

'Help!' shrieked Perfect Peter. 'Help! Help!'

Mum and Dad ran over.

'What's happened?'

'We got attacked by pirates!' wailed Parveen.

'We ran for our lives!' wailed Gordon.

'Pirates?' said Mum.

'Pirates?' said Dad. 'How many were there?'

'Five!'

'Ten!'

'Hundreds!' wailed Mini Minnie.

'Don't be silly,' said Mum.

'I'm sure they're gone now, so let's find the treasure,' said Dad.

Peter opened the map and headed for the hedge nearest to the gate where the treasure map showed a giant X.

'I'm too scared,' he whimpered.

Helpful Hari crept to the treasure chest and lifted the lid. Everyone gasped. All that was left inside were a few crumpled gold wrappers.

'The treasure's gone,' whispered Peter.

Just then Horrid Henry sauntered along the path, twirling his hat.

'Where have you been?' said Mum.

'Hiding,' said Horrid Henry truthfully.

'We got raided,' gasped Ted.

'By pirates,' gasped Gordon.

'No way,' said Horrid Henry.

'They stole all the pieces of eight,' wailed Peter.

Horrid Henry sighed.

'What did I tell you about the cannibal curse?' he said. 'Just be glad you've still got your heads.'

Hmmmm, boy, chocolate pieces of eight were always yummy, but raided pieces of eight tasted even better, thought Horrid Henry that night, shoving a few more chocolates into his mouth.

Come to think of it, there'd been too many pirate parties recently.

Now, a cannibal curse party . . . Hmmmn.

Come to Henry's
Cannibal Curse
Birthday Party

PARTY MENU

Chocolate Eyeballs

Jelly bellies

Liquorice hair

PARTY GAMES

Bobbing for eyeballs

Bash the brain

Bogey-eating contest

Whack the skull off the skeleton

Shrink Peter's head

HORRiD HENRY'S Top Secret Fact File

Best Parties
Pirate parties
Cannibal curse parties
Terminator Gladiator parties

Worst Parties
Sammy the Snail party
Daffy and her Dancing
Daisies party
Princess party

Best Wedding
NONE!

Worst Wedding
Marrying Miss
Battle-Axe

Best Dinner Guests
Terminator Gladiator
Mutant Max
Marvin the Maniac
Tapioca Tina
Rapper Zapper

Worst Dinner Guests

Miss Battle-Axe
Stuck-Up Steve
Demon Dinner Lady

Best Revenge

Telling Peter there were fairies
at the bottom of the garden
Making Peter believe he was
famous in the future
Getting Bossy Bill into trouble
Making Steve think there were
monsters under the bed

Worst Revenge

Peter sending Margaret a letter signed 'Henry' asking
her to marry him (uggh)

Best Hike

Walking between the
comfy black chair
and the fridge

Worst Hike

Anywhere outdoors

Best Sleepovers

Eating all the ice cream at Greedy Graham's
Breaking all the beds at Dizzy Dave's
Staying up all night at Rude Ralph's

Worst Sleepovers

New Nick
Stuck-Up Steve
Moody Margaret nabbing my room

Best Will

Anyone leaving me lots of loot

Worst Will

Mine

Best Restaurants

Gobble and Go
Whopper Whoopee
Fat Frank's

Worst Restaurants

Restaurant Le Posh
Virtuous Veggie